A dude ranch in the Pe: ~~officer~~ who ditches her job rather than foreclose on the family that's run that ranch for generations? A handsome southern he-man who needs an office assistant? How can a city girl resist a Dixie cowboy?

THE OWNER OF the ranch needed an assistant who could handle the reservations, make deposits, pay the company bills, and manage the housekeeping staff. She'd learned all that and more from her numerous degrees in business and finance. She read the ad three times.

This ranch is beautiful. I love it.

Movement from inside the house drew her thoughts back to the reason she waited on the porch. Her father's voice roared inside her head. *Serve those foreclosure papers, or find another job.* Her gaze snapped to the message board and zoned in on the want ad. *If only.*

The incredibly sexy cowboy who had originally greeted her when she'd arrived at the Dixie Rooster Ranch pulled the door open.

"I'm sorry about the wait. My uncle needed my help." Over his broad shoulder Katy saw an elderly man in a wheelchair coming toward them down a long hallway. Since his leg was elevated and in a cast she presumed she was about to come face to face with the soon-to-be evicted Frank Davis.

He rolled his chair through the open doors, and, once on the porch, he extended his hand to Katy. "Hi, there. I take it you're the reporter from the *Cantor Gazette*?"

Confused, Katy stammered for a second, then found her voice. "No, sir. I'm Katlyn—"

"Tyler?" Mr. Davis looked at the other man. "Didn't you tell me the reporter from the newspaper was here?"

Tyler shrugged. "I'm sorry, Katlyn."

"Katy." Why had she said that? This wasn't a casual visit to make new friends. She had serious business to attend to. *Katy* made her sound young and inexperienced.

"I'm Tyler Davis." The cowboy shook her hand. "I'll be managing the ranch until Uncle Frank gets back on his feet."

He held her hand longer than necessary. Blood hummed through her veins. Captured by his gaze and lost in the crystal blue of his eyes, she felt their power to the bottom of her stomach.

Begrudgingly, Katy looked from Tyler to Frank Davis to George. Their waiting stares paralyzed her. She literally had to force herself to look away. The logo on the stationery of the want ad beckoned her to glance at it again.

"Well, Katy," Tyler said, "what can we help you with?"

Panic forced a knot in her throat. Impulsively, she ripped the want ad from the message board and then shook it slightly in Tyler's direction. "I want this job."

———

"Dolores Wilson writes a laugh-out-loud tale that will touch your heart and leave you wanting more."
—*Kathie DeNosky, USA TODAY Bestselling Author*

Dixie Cowboy

Book 1 of The Dixie Cowboys Series

by

Dolores Wilson

Bell Bridge Books

Bell Bridge Books
PO BOX 300921
Memphis, TN 38130
Print ISBN: 978-1-61194-374-0

Bell Bridge Books is an Imprint of BelleBooks, Inc.

We at BelleBooks enjoy hearing from readers.
Visit our websites – www.BelleBooks.com and
www.BellBridgeBooks.com.

10 9 8 7 6 5 4 3 2 1

Cover design: Debra Dixon
Interior design: Hank Smith
Photo/Art credits:
Scene (manipulated) © chesterf | Depositphotos.com

:Lcdr:01:

Dedication

To my husband Richard, who is my very own Dixie Cowboy.

Chapter 1

"FRANK DAVIS HAS to be kicked off that ranch today." Bill Mays, president of Mays Savings and Loan, made his demand perfectly clear to his chief loan officer and only daughter, Katlyn. Unfortunately, his words were not heard by her alone. Surely her father's thunderous timbre had been audible to everyone throughout the bank and maybe even the parking lot.

"But Dad." Where had that come from? He'd always insisted that while at work, Katy call him *Mr. Mays* just like all the employees did. With that slip of the tongue, her confidence and her shoulders sagged another notch. But why? She'd done her homework. She knew her points were valid. Straightening her spine, she took a deep breath.

"I've studied the file for the Dixie Rooster Ranch and Mr. Davis. He's been injured and can't work to get the ranch ready for the patrons who will be arriving in a few weeks to spend their vacations on a guest ranch." Mercifully her breathing stayed on an even keel. Her voice hadn't cracked a bit. She took that as a green light to continue her argument. "His rotten son sank Mr. Davis deep into debt, then skipped town. That ranch has been in his family for well over a hundred and thirty years. He'll fight hard to heal and be able to turn his situation around. All he needs is time to recover and resume his business, and I'm sure he'll be able to make his payments."

Her father's icy expression told her that her argument hadn't dented his resolve, and he was not going to back down from his decision to foreclose.

Katy pulled up her big girl panties and stepped closer to her father's desk. "I'm not going out there and strip that poor man of his life-long home. As chief loan officer, I've made the decision to give him an extension."

Pride in her newly-found courage stiffened her spine, forcing her to stand tall and defiant. Fire in her father's gaze melted all that and turned it into a puddle of goo in the pit of her stomach. She knew that glare well. The wrath that followed would not be pretty.

"Well, Katlyn Tara, allow me to give you a quick lesson in economics. If the bank doesn't collect the money due us, we must take possession of the property and resell as soon as possible. Otherwise, there is no money to pay the bank's employees, which includes you and me."

Her father eased his substantial body into his hunter green leather chair and then rested his forearms on his massive desk.

This was a new demeanor for Katy's father. One she'd never seen before. What happened to the big boom she'd expected because she'd stood up to him? A strange thought zapped her brain. She'd *never* talked back to him or voiced her opposition to anything. The chills zinging through her entire body told her there would be a confrontation, and it was going to turn ugly.

"Katlyn, have you ever stopped to wonder where the money came from for all the expensive clothes your mother made sure you had? What about the small fortune spent on dance lessons, recital clothing, traveling to competitions all over this country? Then the years in beauty contests?" Her father leaned back in his chair and rubbed his chin.

He gave her a moment to respond, but as usual, Katy knew from the few confrontations she'd had with her father, he didn't really want a reply. Eventually, he continued. "Let me tell you where all that came from. It came from doing whatever was necessary to recoup all the money we have loaned, plus interest. And, sometimes to do that, we have to foreclose and resell the property."

His dark eyebrows knitted close together. "If you didn't know that just from growing up around the banking business, didn't you learn that while you were getting all those expensive degrees in finance? Surely the premise of how businesses work should have been discussed in a few of your classes."

"Yes, sir, I do understand that. I just—"

Her dad's extended palm stopped her. "The bottom line is: Get out to the Dixie Rooster Ranch and serve Frank Davis with his thirty-day foreclosure papers or"—his voice hardened even more than it had been—"find yourself another job."

He silently dismissed his daughter with a sweep of his hand. Her weighted legs threatened to drop her on the spot. Thankfully, she made it through the doorway, to her desk to pick up Frank Davis' file, then left the bank. But on the long walk across the parking lot, tears spilled from her eyes and burned trails into the expensive makeup her mother had insisted she wear since the day she'd turned sixteen. Expensive makeup bought with money her father had made sometimes at the expense of other people.

Of course Katy knew all that, but since her first day on the job two years prior at Mays Savings and Loan she dealt with people who trusted her with their money, like processing loans for small businesses or new homes, helping deserving people to reach their dreams. Katy loved that part. But there was so much more to it. And those were the things that stabbed Katy's heart in ways she knew she could never accept.

But there she was, speeding her red Lexus over a country road leading to the Dixie Rooster Ranch. No matter how much it threatened to break her heart, Katy would have to do her job, or she'd have to find another one. She only hoped she could get through it without turning into a quivering mass.

AT LONG LAST, the gates of the Dixie Rooster Ranch came into view. Beyond them a huge, two-story, log cabin rose above a lush emerald green lawn which sloped gently to the rushing water of a wide creek. Katy drove through the open gates and then followed the dusty road leading to the main house and lined on both sides with pink crepe myrtle trees. As the car bumped over the rough wooden bridge, Katy's stomach did a violent roll, and for a moment, she thought she would lose her breakfast.

She'd only had to execute one other foreclosure during her

banking career. That was the day she'd helped police set eighty-year-old Lucy Jamison's belongings on the curb because she hadn't paid taxes for a few years. Ten to be exact.

Back then, Katy calmed the angry sea inside her by begging her friend, Maria, to allow Lucy to stay in Maria's home until the elderly woman's daughter could drive to Cantor, Georgia, from Los Angeles, two long weeks later. Katy had taken care of all of Lucy's expenses and thought she might have to make the woman one of her tax exemptions, when her daughter finally arrived.

During the time she spent with Lucy Jamison, Katy had received several pieces of sage advice, but one played over in her mind more times than any other—*You can live your life doing exactly what's expected of you, then die. Or, you can live it to the fullest doing the right thing, and then die. Which one would you rather do?*

Katy's answer would be to the fullest, of course. But exactly what did that mean?

While deeply pondering that question, Katy pulled into Frank Davis' front yard. Directly in front of her, she saw a male's behind sticking from under the hood of an old truck. A large rip in the seat of his pants exposed underwear, decorated with Tweety, no less. Her gaze slowly drifted from the well-defined, masculine behind down to the hem of his coveralls, which rose a good two inches above his socks.

Must be expecting a flood.

Katy nipped her bottom lip between her teeth. Her regard for the man's backside intensified. Its perfection could not belong to sixty-something Frank Davis. A handyman, perhaps?

He spun around and caught her staring. She bit her lip hard, and heat rose to the top of her head. She choked back her embarrassment and climbed out of her car. Slamming the door, she started toward the man. A big, long-eared bloodhound charged in her direction, stopping only a few feet from her.

She came to a fast halt and sucked in a quick breath. "Will he bite?" She hoped not.

"I don't know. Come on up, and we'll find out." The man spoke with a slight drawl. Not the heavy southern accent Katy heard from most of the customers at the bank.

If he puzzled her at first, the sparkle of mischief in the man's blue eyes reassured her he was joking. She took another step forward. The dog bared his teeth and growled. Racing back into her car, she knocked her head on the door facing.

"George," the man called to the dog. "Get over there and lay down." He pointed to the area in front of a vast porch which wrapped around a major part of the ranch house.

George did as he was told and lumbered across the yard to a shady spot. He plopped onto his stomach, his ears spread onto the grass. The man wiped his hands on a grease-stained rag and made his way to Katy's car door.

Again, she opened it.

"HE'S REALLY HARMLESS, just a little protective." Tyler Davis extended his hand to the pretty lady. She hesitated for a moment then laid her hand in his open palm. His fingers closed around hers. They were warm and soft, and Tyler liked the way they felt.

He watched the woman with great interest. She swung her long, slender legs out of the car and placed her feet on the ground. He didn't miss the hem of her skirt edging its way upward, exposing creamy white thighs. His gaze moved down past her perfectly shaped calves and trim ankles all the way to her expensive shoes.

With a slight tug, he pulled the woman to her feet. He almost laughed out loud wondering what she would think if he complimented her on her Jimmy Choos or whatever those brands were that Beth Bishop, his back-stabbing ex-fiancée, would pay out the nose for and then spew forth their names like they were supposed to mean something to Tyler.

Regardless of how much they cost, the shoes on the pretty feet in front of him battled with the gravel in the driveway. The woman lost her footing. He took her arm, but she pulled away and steadied herself against the car.

"Are you okay?" he asked.

She pushed by him only to wobble again.

"Here." He took her by the arm, whether she liked it or not, and walked her safely to the edge of the driveway and onto the grass which he noticed desperately needed mowing. Another chore to be added to things to do. The list grew longer and was quickly getting out of control. Killing his no-good cousin topped the list.

"Do you happen to know how many years a guy could get for murder in Georgia?" Tyler smiled, and the woman stared, mouth agape. A look of terror made a rapid appearance across her face and forced any hint of sparkle in her eyes to disappear like the last fortune cookie in a Chinese restaurant.

"I'm sorry." Tyler tried not to laugh. "I was just kidding. Honest." He cleared his throat to disguise the humor he'd found in his own words and averted his gaze from the swell of her breast to the curve of her mouth. Suddenly he had a strong desire to draw her into his arms and calm her apparent uneasiness with a well-executed kiss.

A glint of sunlight reflected off the red Lexus the well-dressed, sexy-legged, beautiful-mouthed woman had driven to the ranch. Thankfully, a distraction. It was exactly the make and model his girlfriend Beth—make that back-stabbing ex-girlfriend—had bought with some of the commission money she'd gotten for the ad campaign she'd stolen from Tyler.

He glanced down and realized his rudeness in ignoring the woman was unacceptable. "The sun must be baking my brain. You're here on business, and I'm keeping you from it."

The man towered a good eight or nine inches above Katy. She looked up into his crystal blue eyes.

A loud, buzzer-type bell rang out in earsplitting decibels. Katy gasped and sprang forward against his hard chest. He was too close, and, despite his rag-tag looks, he smelled great. A subtle musk with a hint of motor oil.

Jeez, Katlyn get your mind on business, please.

"Sorry," she mumbled and tried her best to regain the decorum she needed to take care of the dreaded chore that lay ahead. "Since you don't appear to have a broken leg, I assume you are not Frank Davis."

The man shook his head. "No, I'm—"

The buzzer rang again. He spun on his heels and then called over his shoulder. "That's Uncle Frank letting me know he needs me." When he reached the two steps leading to the massive porch, he stopped and turned to face her. "With his leg busted, I have to help him with almost everything. Please come on up. I'll be right back."

Katy made her way to the porch, keeping her gaze ever steady on good old George. The dog rose in a ho-hum way and followed her up the steps. She moved to the front door of the cabin. George flopped down on the wooden porch and exhaled an exasperated sigh as if to say his work was done, or he was just too darn tired to be bothered.

To the right of the door, a cork message board had been attached to the logs of the cabin's outer wall. Brochures, announcements, business cards of various establishments of the local community decorated the entire board. On a light beige sheet of ranch stationery, Katy saw an interesting ad.

The owner of the ranch needed an assistant who could handle the reservations, make deposits, pay the company bills, and manage the housekeeping staff. She'd learned all that and more from her numerous degrees in business and finance. She read the ad three times. With each pass, she knew she could do that job with little effort at all.

When she thought back to her college days, she knew in her heart she'd continued her education to delay the inevitable. Eventually, her father caught on to the fact that Katy would go for a degree in what he called *"Hockyology"*—analyzing dog poop—if it kept her from actually going to work for her demanding father. Katy gave her head a gentle shake to chase away any more negative thoughts. She faced enough as it was.

From where she stood on the front porch of the main house, a gorgeous, panoramic view spread out in all directions. Four large buildings appeared to be two-story bunk houses. The wonderful smell of fresh, clean air with a hint of late-blooming peach blossoms floated around her. The essence corralled her rapidly spinning mind and calmed her troubled soul like nothing she could ever remember.

Katy gave only a cursory thought to what might be keeping the man. She would hang on to the peace she'd just experienced for as long as possible. A fair distance from the house, she could see a stable and, beyond that, several more horses in a beautiful green pasture. Katy couldn't remember the last time she'd ridden a horse. Her mother didn't think it was a ladylike activity for her precious daughter, but she rode her friend Maria's Tennessee Walker every time Katy visited. She could almost hear the creak of the leather saddle and feel the wind whipping through her long hair. Her mother would have had a fit if she'd seen her.

"You have a beautiful place here, George."

Hearing his name, the bloodhound got up and then strolled over to her. He looked up at her with sad eyes. Sensing she had made a friend, she scratched the velvety fur behind his ear. Waves of compassion banded her heart. They were strange feelings to Katy. She'd never been allowed to have a pet. Her mother forbade any "filthy beasts" to enter their home. Surprisingly, George warmed Katy's heart and put a smile on her face.

Movement from inside the house drew her thoughts back to the reason she waited on the porch. Her father's voice roared inside her head. *Serve those papers, or find another job.* Her gaze snapped to the message board and zoned in on the want ad. *If only.*

The man who had originally greeted her when she'd arrived at the Dixie Rooster Ranch pulled the door open.

"I'm sorry about that. My uncle needed my help." Over his shoulder Katy saw an elderly man in a wheelchair coming toward them down a long hallway. Since his leg was elevated and in a cast she presumed she was about to come face to face with the soon-to-be evicted Frank Davis.

He rolled his chair through the open doors and once on the porch, he extended his hand to Katy. "Hi there. I take it you're the reporter from the *Cantor Gazette?*"

Confused, Katy stammered for a second, then found her voice. "No, sir. I'm Katlyn—"

"Tyler?" Mr. Davis looked at the other man. "Didn't you tell me the reporter from the newspaper was here?"

Tyler shrugged. "I'm sorry, Katlyn."

"Katy." Why had she said that? This wasn't a casual visit to make new friends. She had serious business to attend to. *Katy* made her sound young and inexperienced.

"I'm Tyler Davis." He shook her hand. "I'll be managing the ranch until Uncle Frank gets back on his feet."

He held her hand longer than necessary. Blood hummed through her veins. Captured by his gaze and lost in the crystal blue of his eyes, she felt their power to the bottom of her stomach.

Begrudgingly, Katy looked from Tyler to Frank Davis to George. Their waiting stares paralyzed her. She literally had to force herself to look away. The logo on the stationery of the want ad beckoned her to glance at it again.

"Well, Katy," Tyler said, "what can we help you with?"

Panic forced a knot in her throat. Impulsively, she ripped the want ad from the message board and then shook it slightly in Tyler's direction. "I want this job."

Chapter 2

WOW! JUST EXACTLY what had hit Tyler Davis square in the gut and left his head spinning? As close as he could tell, it was a five-foot-four, piercing brown-eyed whirlwind named Katy. And somewhere between *hello* and *I want this job*, he'd lost all business sense and hired the pretty lady just because she wanted the job. Was it because she turned him into a seventeen-year-old with raging hormones?

Darn, he hadn't even asked her last name. Didn't know where she hailed from, and, most importantly, didn't know if she had the skills needed to be his assistant. She dressed in very expensive clothes and looked like she'd been put together by a Hollywood make-up artist and stylist, but how would that work into the ranch life? How were her phone skills? Did she even have any? Could she balance a checkbook? She was awfully skittish. Would she be able to meet and greet and assist the guests, or would she mumble her way through every conversation?

"Don't look at me like that, George," Tyler scolded the long-eared dog. "I've seen you chasing Mr. Moro's border collie. You know exactly how I got into this mess. Now, I need you to help me figure out how to get out of it." He reached down and ruffled the fur on the dog's back.

"Let's go, boy." Tyler marched down the steps and into the yard. "I have to go check on the two guys painting the last bunkhouses." George lumbered down the stairs beside Tyler, but when his feet touched the plush grass, he flopped onto his belly for an afternoon nap.

Tyler glanced around, then laughed. "Okay, you rest, boy. I'll be back to feed you and Uncle Frank lunch in just a few minutes."

With all the work he had to do, Tyler buried himself in the next few tasks on his list. But none of them kept his gaze from periodically returning to the dusty road leading to the ranch house. Katy had assured Tyler she would go pick up some of her belongings and be back before suppertime. He looked for a dust cloud on the horizon to signal his new live-in assistant had returned. Katy . . . Katy . . . what's-her-name.

KATY MAYS SLUMPED over the steering wheel of her car. She'd been sitting in the driveway of her parents' house, the place where she'd grown up and continued to call home.

The old Victorian house held six bedrooms and three baths. She'd had the bedroom on the third floor with adjoining bathroom and her own sitting area. Since her days as a carefree teenager, she'd pretended she lived alone, but for all of her twenty-eight years, she'd never really done that.

Her parents had always been right there. Even in college she'd shared a dorm room with three other sorority sisters. Solitude was never an option. And, for the past few years, all her free time had been spent with Jeremy Everson.

But that was about to change, and the ramifications of her rebellion would surely come back to bite her in the butt.

Katy checked her watch. Oh, no. She had to hurry. Her mom would be home from her once-a-week bridge game in about half an hour. Katy rushed inside and up the back staircase to her room. She pulled two large suitcases from her walk-in closet and opened them on the bed.

Now would come the hard part. What did she own that would be appropriate to wear for her new position as Tyler Davis' personal assistant? Rifling through her hanging clothes, she could find only three blouses that didn't smack of society girl. She did find a few pairs of jeans and a couple of Capri pants, ones she'd worn when she'd gone to visit her friend Maria.

"Maria. Of course." Katy pulled her cell phone from her skirt pocket and rapidly punched in the number.

"Hello." Maria's bubbly voice lifted Katy's spirits.

"I need your help." She hadn't meant to sound so frantic, but since she truly was, she couldn't hold it back. "Can you come to my house and pick me up and then take me to a ranch out in Carteret? I'll buy you gas, but I have to leave now."

"Good heavens. I'll be right there, but you got a whole lot of explaining to do."

That was so true, but before Katy did another thing she had to explain everything to her mom. That struck more than terror in her tumbling stomach. It struck pain in her heart. Her mother had such high hopes for her only daughter. She'd made sure Katy had the best of everything, even down to the finest stationery to send out proper hand-written letters like all well-mannered ladies should do.

"Where's that pearl-white stationery Mom bought a few weeks ago?" Katy found it and sat down to write her parents a letter. She knew full well this wasn't what her mother had in mind for her expensive stationery.

Dear Mom and Dad,

I hope you are not too disappointed with me, but I've decided to make a career change. This morning Dad said that, if I couldn't serve foreclosure papers then I should find another job. I thought a lot about that, and I know for sure I don't have the stomach for that kind of business world.

I'm taking a little time to get my act together and decide what I want to do. If you don't hear from me for a while, please don't worry. I'm a big girl, and I can take care of myself.

Daddy, I am leaving my Lexus here. I know it was my college graduation present because you were expecting me to work for you at the bank. Sorry I wasn't better suited for the job.

I'll be in touch as soon as I work through the what-do-I-want-to-be-when-I-grow-up issue.

I love you both, and I thank you from the bottom of my heart for everything.

Love,

Katlyn

Katy threw the last of the things she thought she would need for her new job into the suitcases. She'd dragged them down the stairs, each hitting the tread with a *thump*. Earlier, on her way upstairs, she had placed Frank Davis' foreclosure file on the breakfast table. Now, she laid the envelope containing the letter to her parents on top of the file. For a moment, she couldn't let go of it. Sadness pierced her heart, and she nearly changed her mind, but that passed quickly. She was making a move from her familiar world to something so foreign it could just as well be on the other side of the world. Suddenly, a charge of excitement rippled over her skin. She searched her mind for the positive side of her decision and, much to her surprise, found it in the middle of newly-found independence—she'd never have to hurt or disappoint anyone again by denying a loan or throwing them out of the house.

A loud blast of a car horn pulled her from her melancholy thoughts and propelled her out the door where Maria waited to take her to her new home and hopefully, the beginning of a new and exciting life.

TYLER HEARD THE gravel crunching under tires in the driveway. He wiped his hands on the dishtowel he'd just used to clean up the kitchen after fixing his and Uncle Frank's lunch. He flung the towel on the counter and hurried to the front door.

His new assistant pulled two huge suitcases from the trunk of a late model car driven by a pretty, dark-haired woman.

Wonder what happened to the nice red sled she'd driven earlier?

"Wait." He tromped down the steps and made it to the car just as Katy sat the last suitcase on the ground. "I'll take those." Tyler lifted both bags and then moved to the edge of the grass. He started to ask what happened to her car, but she was leaning through the open passenger's window, talking to the person who had brought her back to the ranch.

Trying to avert his attention from the curve of Katy's backside, Tyler glanced out into the deep, green meadow, but that didn't last long. His gaze preferred the treat of the closer view. He'd thought his ex, Beth, had a cute rear, but this gal far outranked her in the sexy department.

"Darn," he muttered under his breath. Even though he and Beth Bishop had broken off their two-year relationship three weeks earlier, just the thought of her still brought the sting of her betrayal to the pit of his stomach.

How could I have been so stupid?

By the time Tyler pulled himself back from the less than happy world he'd left in New York, Katy stood near him, eyeing him as if she might be rethinking her decision to work with him. Before she had a chance to say anything, he snatched up the bags and headed to the house.

"Let's get you settled in, and then we'll go for a tour of the ranch."

Katy followed him onto the porch. She noticed he'd changed from the torn overalls to a pair of jeans. Tight-fitting jeans, and she liked the way they looked from behind. After holding the door open for him, she trailed behind him into a large sitting area that held a registration desk and a huge fireplace surrounded by flat stones. Her new boss stomped down a long hallway. She hurried to catch up. Checking out the large bookshelves loaded with hundreds of books would have to wait.

There were several closed doors on both sides of the corridor. Since Katy followed closely on Tyler's heels, she didn't have time to speculate about what might be behind door number one, number two, or number three. She figured she'd learn what each one held in due time.

"This is it. Like I told you earlier, your room and board are included with the job. Right now we are working with a skeleton crew, and they are mostly doing renovations to the bunkhouses. So, you're on your own as far as fixing yourself something to eat." Tyler lifted the bags onto the bed. He turned to a door right behind him and opened it. "This walk-in closet was Aunt Hilda's pride and joy. It's pretty big." He glanced back at her suitcases. "I'm guessing you won't fill it up." The corners of his mouth turned into a radiant smile.

Amusement danced in his eyes. Katy's stomach flipped big time. Pretending to examine the exquisite carving on one of the posts of the rice bed which was the focal point of the room, she steadied herself on weak knees.

Weak knees? Was someone kidding her? She'd seen knock-out smiles up close and personal before, but none had ever had this effect on her. What exactly was it that made this one different? She wasn't sure, but she knew she'd have to keep it under control.

"This was your aunt's bed?" Katy followed through with her little charade of hiding her reaction to him.

"Yes, hers and Uncle Frank's. She passed away almost six years ago." Tyler moved around the room, checking bureau drawers to be sure nothing had been left behind. Katy watched him, but found no sign of anxiety you would expect to see when foreclosure lay just around the bend.

"I don't want to take Mr. Davis' bed."

"Oh, that's not the case at all. He moved into one of the guest rooms down the hall. He said this one was too frou-frou for him, but we all knew it was because his wife of fifty-four years wasn't here anymore."

Katy did a quick scan of the room. Taking into consideration that Priscilla curtains dressed the windows, night stands and dressers were covered with lacy doilies, and the three hurricane table lamps were decorated with tiny blue roses, the room was almost too frou-frou for Katy. The six or more lace-covered pillows resting against the headboard really pushed it over the top.

She turned to Tyler, who was assessing her. "This room looks like it came out of Georgia's Lifestyles of the Rich and Famous."

A soft laugh escaped from Katy's perfect lips.

The sound sent a buzz of electricity through Tyler and

stopped him dead. What was there about this woman's laugh that melted his insides and forced him to take a deep breath? Did it remind him of Beth's laugh? A harsh thought flashed through his mind. He'd heard her laugh so few times; he couldn't remember what she sounded like.

Tyler opened another door and flipped on a light inside the room. "This is your bathroom. There's a door in here that goes into the kitchen, but you can keep it locked. Aunt Hilda used to slip through there and get an early start on breakfast." He unlocked a raised panel door and led the way into a large, farmhouse-style kitchen. He turned to make sure she was following him and nearly knocked her over.

"Oops. Sorry about that." He wasn't really. Their closeness gave Tyler a chance to inhale the sweet scent of her perfume. He guessed something very expensive since he recognized it as one he recalled from Beth's high society circle.

"Carlotta has agreed to come back to work as our cook once it gets closer to the time to reopen the ranch, but until then you can make yourself at home and eat whatever you can find in the fridge and the pantry." Moving quickly, he gave her the ten-cent tour of the kitchen. He opened and closed cabinets, the pantry, and the refrigerator with exaggerated gestures.

I could give Vanna a run for her money. Tyler chuckled to himself.

"Let me know if there is something you would like to have, and we'll add it to the shopping list."

He led the way through the bathroom and back into the bedroom. "Oh, that reminds me, I might need you to do the shopping over the next few weeks. Hope that won't be a problem." He didn't give her time to answer. "By the way, what happened to your jazzy car?"

For just a second, Katy's eyes closed. When she opened them again, her gaze didn't quite meet his. Instead, she kept it trained on her finger tracing the cording on her suitcase. "It wasn't mine. I'm sorry I didn't realize I would need a car as part of my job."

"Oh, you don't." She straightened, and Tyler was sure he saw relief in her eyes. "You can use Old Blue out there. He looks rough, but he drives great."

Katy looked in the direction where he pointed through one of the windows. "Old Blue?"

"Yeah, the truck I was working on when you first came up this morning." He waited for any negative reaction. But none came.

"Yes, of course, Old Blue and I will get along just fine."

Katy's voice lacked the enthusiasm Tyler had hoped for, but he let it pass.

"When we talked this morning, you said you had office experience." He leaned against the door jamb and watched the sunbeams dance through her auburn hair. "Let's narrow that down. Are you comfortable answering phones?"

"Very much so."

"That's good. Can you balance checkbooks, handle accounts receivable and payable?" She nodded.

"Have you ever worked in reservations or guest services in a hotel or a motel?" He held in an uncertain breath.

"No, I haven't done that type of work."

Tyler exhaled loudly.

"But I'm great with people." Again Katy laughed with the sweet sound that immediately put Tyler at ease.

"Here's the deal," she said. "I have a business degree from Emory University. I've worked in finance for a few years, and I don't like it. I thought I'd try my hand at another line of work." Katy removed a small pillow from the bed and stroked it like it was a kitten.

When she looked up at him, Tyler's first thought was that she was evaluating him. She had a story to tell, but she wasn't quite sure of him. He smiled, hoping to put her at ease.

Katy cleared her throat. "To be honest with you, when I said I wanted the job, I didn't know and didn't care if it was washing dishes or mucking out the barns. I just wanted something new." She replaced the pillow and moved around the bed coming to a stop in front of Tyler. "Although I wasn't in the hotel service, I'm a quick study. I'm proficient in computers, public relations, finance, and I can even manage to answer a phone without saying, 'Can I help you some way or 'nother?'"

With what appeared to be little effort, Katy smiled widely, and her brown eyes sharpened.

"Since you hired me so quickly and without my submitting to a skills test, or drug test, or having a list of references, I have to assume you are pretty desperate for help." Her bright eyes darkened, leaving Tyler to wonder why. "Just so you know, I need this job as much as you need an assistant. Management for any line of business has a similar basis, and I know I can either learn with minimal guidance or figure it out on my own. I'll work hard to prove myself."

"I can't ask for more than that." He shoved away from the door jamb. "So, you like your room okay?

"This is all very nice," Katy said. "It's much more than I expected."

"Glad you like it." Tyler meant that. Although it wasn't his, he was very proud of the ranch that had once belonged to his grandparents. He had lived right there in that house until he was six. Then the world as he knew it exploded in unimaginable ways. "Since you will be involved in handling the income and disbursements, I'll need to fill you in on what's been going on during the last few months. Tomorrow, I have to go into downtown Cantor and pay a visit to the bank that holds the mortgage on this place.

"Some high and mighty loan officer named K. T. Mays is breathing foreclosure threats down Uncle Frank's neck. I have to try to talk some sense into the old geezer who evidently has a vault lock where his heart should be. I'll bring you up to speed on all that while I show you around. Why don't you change out of your fancy duds and get into some more suitable for the muck and the mire of the ranch. I'll wait for you in the office next to the registration desk."

Tyler started out the door, but quickly turned back. "I'll get all your information later, but I want to at least get your name posted to our payroll system. I know that Katy is short for Katlyn, but what's your last name?"

Chapter 3

"MY LAST NAME? It's May . . . son." The lie spilled past Katy's lips easier than she would have liked. But she didn't dare tell Tyler her real name. *"Katlyn Mason."*

Tyler had just shown Katy where her quarters would be. It was perfect for her, but just as he was leaving, he ruined the magic of the room by asking her for her full name. Now she wondered how long it would be before he found out the truth about her and sent her sailing into the street.

"Come on up to the office when you are ready." Tyler eased the door of her new room closed.

Well, Katlyn Mason, you are knee deep in it now.

Katy shook her head in hopes of scattering the kaleidoscope images rolling in her mind. She didn't want to think about what would happen when her new boss discovered she is the K. T. Mays whose job, at one time, was to snatch the ranch right out from under him and his uncle. She'd face that issue when the time came. Until then, she would work hard and hopefully become an asset to the Dixie Rooster Ranch. So much so that the Davises would forgive her white lie and ultimately be lost without her.

At least she had a plan, well-defined or not.

Katy pulled a blue pair of Capri pants and a periwinkle and white polka-dotted blouse from her suitcase. Quickly, she shinnied out of the skirt and blouse she'd put on when she left home early that morning. Then she had dressed like a banker, ready to do her banker job. Now, a mere seven hours later, ranch casual transformed her into a cowboy's assistant.

Yee Haw!

With her blue canvas shoes tied and a fresh application of Yves Saint Laurent Pink Celebration applied to her lips, Katy figured she was as ready as she would ever be. She pulled her cell phone from her discarded skirt pocket, checked it for missed calls, and found four as well as six voicemails. She knew she would have to eventually answer at least her mother's, but for now she didn't want to talk to her parents.

As she stared at the phone, it vibrated in her hand. After a quick glance at the caller ID, she turned it off and shoved it into her pants pocket. She didn't want to talk to anyone right then, especially her soon-to-be ex-boyfriend, Jeremy Everson.

IN AN OFFICE just off the receptionist area, Katy found Tyler digging through a file drawer. As he moved from one section to the next, he appeared more and more frustrated.

"Darn." He slammed the drawer with a teeth-jarring *bang*.

Katy thought she should back out of the doorway, but it was too late. Tyler saw her.

"Sorry 'bout that. It's going to take a miracle to clean up the financial mess that my lazy, stupid cousin left behind." He rounded the massive desk piled high with paperwork and gently took Katy's elbow. As he led her through the lobby and out the front door, Tyler never released his hold on her arm.

His touch sent welcoming warmth coursing through her veins. The sensation also caused a stab of guilt, and she knew exactly why. Never had Jeremy's touch caused her stomach to quiver in such a delightful way.

In her heart she knew she never loved Jeremy, but her father wanted him for a son-in-law. Katy had accepted things the way they were because she never wanted to disappoint her father, and until today, disobeying his wishes was something she didn't even care to think about. But as of ten o'clock that morning, she knew she would never go back to the banking business. And she'd never be Mrs. Jeremy Everson.

As they crossed the gravel driveway, Tyler kept his hand on Katy's arm, warming the skin beneath his touch. She hadn't pulled away, but she did ease out of his reach once they stopped in front of bunkhouse number one.

"This is one of three buildings used as guest quarters. There are four rooms upstairs and four on the ground levels." Tyler opened the closest door and then stepped back for Katy to enter. "Our capacity is sixty guests."

She ran her finger over the top of a rough-hewn chest of drawers. Tyler had the distinct feeling she was examining the craftsmanship more than the layers of dust covering all the surfaces in the room. But he wondered how it would feel to have her fingers running over his skin.

"This is very nice," Katy said.

"Uncle Frank built that. As a matter of fact, he built most of the furniture in the main house and the guest houses during the time he and Aunt Hilda ran the ranch. What he didn't build, my grandfather and even my dad built." Tyler's throat constricted slightly. He wondered if Katy had noticed.

"He's very talented." She continued to study the other furniture pieces in the room.

Evidently she hadn't noticed the slip in his composure. He cleared his throat. "They were all very talented.

"This particular room is my favorite. It's where I always stayed when I came back to the ranch for summer vacations." Tyler slid the curtains back and threw open the window. "It all needs airing and cleaning, but it'll be about three weeks before housekeeping and the kitchen staff comes back to work."

Katy moved to the window and stared through it. "Beautiful view. What will go on during the next three weeks?"

"Miramar Technology has reserved the whole ranch for a retreat for some of their employees. They put down a nice deposit, which should have been used to finish up the repairs and maintenance. There are only four weeks left before they arrive. The ranch isn't ready, and Uncle Frank is short on the funds to finish preparing for the guests. But we all know what happened to that money, don't we?" Tyler went outside and headed around the bunkhouse.

"I'm sorry." Not until he heard her speak did he realize Katy had followed close behind him. "I don't know what happened to *that* money."

Tyler slowed until she caught up with him. "My cousin Sidney had borrowed money from the bank in town and had done most of the repairs to reopen the ranch. It had been closed for about six years because, after Aunt Hilda's death, Uncle Frank didn't want to deal with it anymore. Sidney convinced him he would take care of all the work if Uncle Frank would borrow money to get it up and running again." Tyler rubbed the back of his neck, hoping to ease some of the fierce tension gripping him every time he thought of Sid.

"My guess would be that until he broke his leg, Uncle Frank was overseeing everything, and when it fell back on Sid the Snake, he took the deposit made by Miramar and what was left in Uncle Frank's bank account and skipped town."

"That's terrible."

"No, the terrible part is the fact that old man Mays from the bank is going to foreclose and put my uncle out of the only home he's ever known." Tyler shuddered.

"I'm sorry."

Katy's soft voice blanketed Tyler and instantly softened his mood. "You don't have anything to be sorry for. None of this is your doings."

After a quick tour of the guest quarters, Tyler showed Katy around the stable and corral. The muck and mire of those areas didn't seem to faze her. Tyler couldn't begin to picture his ex tromping through the mud in that way. She'd be too concerned with getting her expensive shoes dirty.

"I'm a little confused." Katy put her hand to her forehead to shade the sun from her beautiful brown eyes. Tyler stepped to the side slightly to block the bright rays from her face. "Where were you when your uncle and cousin were trying to get the ranch ready to reopen? Couldn't you do anything to stop him from sinking the property into the depths of foreclosure?"

"By the time I knew anything was wrong, it was too late for me to do anything but pack up and come down here to try to bring order to the chaos."

"Come down here from where?"

"New York. After my father was killed here on the ranch

when a large bull crushed him, my mom moved us north to be close to her family. After that I only got to visit during the summer months when school was out. She hated letting me come here."

"Why?"

"I was all she had left, and she was afraid a massive animal would crush me to death like it had done my father. If she'd seen me bronco riding or herding cattle, she'd probably have had a heart attack." He started walking again. "Come on. I need to feed the horses."

"Is your mother still with you?" Katy asked, falling into step behind him.

"We don't live in the same city, but we see each other often. She's just learned to Skype." A soft chuckle emanated from him. "We also talk on the phone every day. She remarried and has a great husband."

A dose of real life shook Katy a little. She couldn't visualize her mother with anyone but her father. Yet for a short moment, she wondered if her mother would be happier with someone else. Internally she shook that notion from her brain. That was so far beyond her imagination, she couldn't even think about it.

Anxious to find another avenue of thought, she continued with her personal, and probably unprofessional, line of questions. "What about you? Are you married? Have any kids?"

"Not yet." Just outside the stable, Tyler patted a horse on the rump. It flicked its tail then turned enough to bump Katy with its muzzle. She scratched the horse's ear and stroked its mane. It had been a long time since she'd done that, but it quickly reminded her of happy times her family knew nothing about. A time when she would visit her friend's farm. She and Maria would ride through the meadows, allowing the wind to clear her mind of the structured life she led at home.

While Katy had been daydreaming, Tyler had moved into the stable. She hurried to catch up with him. She wanted to know more about the handsome man who had the ability to make her heart do a flip by merely looking at her.

Tyler scooped some kind of fodder into a bucket attached

to one of the doors of a stall. A tall chestnut horse snorted then quickly began eating. Anything Katy knew about horses she had learned from Maria. It pleased her to show off her knowledge in front of her new boss.

"She's a fine Tennessee Walker."

"Huh? Oh, yeah. Her name is Shiloh." Tyler moved on down the line, feeding two more horses.

Katy noticed a possible distraction in his voice. "Do you ride?" she asked.

"I don't have time for things like that."

Tapping into Tyler's secret world proved harder than she thought. She'd put too many variables into one question. Was he married? Did he have kids? He'd answered, *not* yet, but that left her wondering exactly what that meant. Did that mean he was married and didn't have any kids yet? Or, did it mean he had a woman in New York waiting for him to come back? Oddly, the idea of another woman tightened her insides with a pang of jealousy.

At first the question of what he did for a living never entered her mind because she thought he lived and worked on his uncle's dude ranch. Evidently, since he lived in New York, that wasn't the case, but she would never have guessed he didn't live there. He certainly looked the part of a ranch hand.

She stood quietly and watched him gather a couple of shovels and rakes and put them in their proper places on a cypress plank wall just outside a room which stored tack. He appeared lost in his own thoughts.

They were just leaving the stable when the buzzer sounded from the house. Katy remembered that was Uncle Frank's signal that he needed Tyler for something.

"Oh, I've got to go check that out. Please feel free to look in any of the guest rooms and the out buildings. As soon as I take care of Uncle Frank, I'll rustle us up some grub." Tyler smiled widely. "How's that for cowboy talk?"

"Works for me." Katy returned the smile and resisted the urge to giggle like a school girl. The tall, handsome man with a smile that melted her insides made her feel like a giddy teenager.

She watched Tyler walk from the stable across the driveway to the main house. She sucked in a lungful of warm Georgia air. There was something about the way he carried himself that called to the woman within her.

Once he'd disappeared inside, she walked the short distance to another two-story bunkhouse. She looked into two different rooms and found they were similar in décor, but allowed for a different number of guests in each. Not far from the bunkhouses, a wide creek gurgled noisily its way past where she stood and disappeared under the bridge she'd crossed as she had driven up the driveway. The sound wrapped her in a way she'd seldom experienced. Peaceful and calming.

She checked her watch. Five thirty-five. The late afternoon sun streaked pink and yellow through the sky. It nearly took Katy's breath away. Had the onset of evening always been that beautiful? Had Katy never taken the time to appreciate nature's wonders? As much as she hated to admit it, she really hadn't looked beyond the fancy clothes, the sports cars, and extravagant vacations all paid for by her father in exchange for her working in a profession she really wasn't cut out for and despised more than she could ever relate to her father.

As a result, she had never stopped to smell the proverbial roses. Maybe she could change that starting that very day. Katy reached down and plucked a purple daisy-like flower growing wildly along the creek bank. She stuck it to her nose and promptly sneezed. Maybe not.

Katy pulled her cell phone from her pocket and turned it on. She might as well get the hard stuff over and call her mom. She punched in the number and took a deep breath. Her mom answered almost before the first ring finished.

"Katlyn, where are you?" Her mom's voice sounded more worried than angry.

"That doesn't matter, Mom. I just want you to know I'm fine. I need some time to sort through some things."

"What kind of things?"

"Things like what I want to do with my life, where I really belong, and who I want in my life. Right now, I need to separate myself from things that don't make me happy. Working with Dad at the bank has never done that, and I'm pretty sure it never will. I know I owe you and Dad so much. I'll take care of paying you back for my education, but I intend to use my business degree in a way that is best for me. Please try to be happy for me, and please try to explain it to Dad."

"Your dad is right here. He wants to talk to you."

"No, Mom . . ."

Her dad came on the line. She resisted her first instinct, which was to hang up.

"Katlyn Tara, what in God's name has gotten into you? You have upset your mother in the worst possible way. Now you tell us where you are, and I'll send a cab to bring you home."

"I'm sorry, Daddy, but I'm not coming home. I'll call again in a week or so just to let you know I am okay, but I won't be home until I have my head on straight and my mind on a level ground. Please understand. Tell Mom I love her." She paused and took in a deep breath. "I love you, Daddy. Bye."

She disconnected and clutched the phone to her chest. That had been hard, but standing up for herself had felt good. She strolled slowly in the direction of the bunkhouse. She'd just reached the stable and was stepping around a huge watering trough. Her cell rang. She jerked to a stop and looked at it, fully expecting it to be her father, but that wasn't to be. She raised the phone to her ear.

"Hello, Jeremy."

"Katlyn, just exactly what do you think you are doing? Do you have any idea how much stress you are causing your mother and how much you have disappointed your father?"

"No, Jeremy, I'm so self-absorbed that I can't think of anyone else." Sarcasm dripped from her voice. Katy almost chuckled at the dead silence that came to her through the phone. "Did I steal your thunder, Jeremy? Was that what you wanted to say to me? Well, that's too bad. I'm not going back to my parents' home, I'm not going back to work at the bank, and—"

"You *have* to go back to work." Jeremy's voice literally squeaked.

"No, I don't."

"Yes, you do. Your father has promised to make me the VP after you and I are married."

"Well, I can see how that would put a kink in your long-term career plans, but I can't be concerned with that right now."

"Listen, you need to tell me where you are. I have a foreclosure to serve, and as soon as that's done, I'll come and get you. We need to talk. I'm sure I can help you find some sense in that scattered brain of yours."

Katy had heard all she could. She ended the call and couldn't stop the corners of her mouth from forming a smile. For the first time in a long time, she'd made decisions for herself and didn't really care if anyone else agreed with her. With no thought at all, she dropped the phone into the murky water of the horse trough and started around the bunkhouse in the direction of the main house.

She came to an abrupt halt. Her breath stopped, too. She flattened her back against the side of the building and then only dared to take a quick peek. Parked in the driveway in front of the main house sat a low-slung black sports car. Tyler had evidently heard the car coming and was waiting on the porch. The next time she looked around the corner, her gaze locked with Tyler's. She shook her head in a silent plea to not give her away.

She watched, still not daring to breathe. With each second, her heart sank deeper into despair. She had no way to stop what was happening on the porch of the main house. All she could do was be an unwilling witness as Tyler took what Katy knew were foreclosure papers from the hand of Jeremy Everson.

Chapter 4

GATHERED AROUND the kitchen table, Uncle Frank, Katy and Tyler ate the simple meal he had prepared. Grilled cheese and tomato soup. Gourmet? No. Satisfying? Yes. Tyler stood and collected the saucer and bowl, and Katy took them from him. Their fingers touched lightly. For a fleeting second, the tips of her fingers tingled, making her breath catch. How could a mere touch affect her that way?

"You cooked. I'll do the dishes." She gathered a few more pieces from the table and moved to the sink.

"I do have paperwork that needs my immediate attention. Thanks." Tyler pulled Uncle Frank's wheelchair away from the table and rolled him out into the hallway, but stopped quickly. "Where to?" he asked.

Frank pointed to his left in the direction of the sitting area. "Think I'll watch a little television."

"Excellent choice." Once Tyler had his uncle settled, he handed him the remote. "I'll be in the office, if you need me." Tyler grinned behind the old man's back. Frank would soon be lost in one of the many *Cops* reruns. He wouldn't need anything for a little while.

Tyler sank down onto a brown leather office chair. Badly worn, the leather showed the battle scars of the years of use Frank had given it during his long run as the ranch owner. Tyler liked the way his bottom fit against the old cowhide. Much more comfortable than the expensive Natuzzi leather on his chair in his office back in New York City.

He'd never wanted anything so extravagant, but Beth would settle for nothing less. But that was the way Beth felt about everything. The most expensive showed what she was worth. Put a price tag on it, and that elevated your worth in the eyes of the world. So different from Tyler's way of thinking.

After living together for two years, Tyler should have known better than to think she would accept the ring his father had given his mother when they became engaged. No, she would settle for nothing less than a huge diamond sparkling to the tune of thirty thousand dollars. The major part of his savings.

Tyler slid a wooden letter opener under the seal of an envelope. Separate stacks of bills appeared to be having babies. There were many, and Tyler had no idea how he would be able to pay them. He'd been using the remainder of his savings to keep the electricity on, buy food, and pay the few workers who labored to get the ranch in shape for paying guests who were due to arrive for a company retreat in less than a month.

Now the foreclosure papers glaring at him from the center of the cluttered desk churned his insides and painfully squeezed his heart. Unless he could talk the high and mighty K. T. Mays into giving him extra time, at the end of the month, the expected guests would be welcomed by a ghost ranch.

Looking at the official bank papers brought a vivid picture to his mind. His new assistant had hidden behind the barn when she saw the arrogant man who had served the papers to Tyler. There was a connection, and Tyler would find out what that was very soon.

He stared at the disarray on the desk until his vision blurred. He blinked and cleared away the bleariness. Across the desk from him stood a welcoming sight—Katy.

"Oh, hi." Tyler cleared his throat and wondered how long she'd been standing there. "Is there something I can do for you?"

"Actually, I was wondering if I could be of some help to you."

"You say you have a business degree, right?"

"Yes, I do."

"Tomorrow I'd like you to go through all this mail and papers and see if you can make some sense of it." He straightened several stacks, but realized the uselessness of his action.

"I can certainly do that." Katy's mouth formed a perfect smile.

Tyler felt an overwhelming desire to kiss it. *Whoa.* He needed to put a stop to that kind of thinking right away. He certainly didn't want to take a chance of running off the only hope he had of getting some sort of organization to the overtaxed desk.

"Would you like me to start tonight?" Katy's tongue licked at her lips.

Tyler stared at her mouth for a second, then gave himself a mental shake hoping to jar his inappropriate thoughts away. He rose. "No, it's been here this long. It'll wait until morning." Once he had rounded the desk, he lightly touched her elbow and guided her out of the office. "Would you mind joining me on the front porch?"

"Of course not." Even before he spoke, she knew he would be questioning her about Jeremy and why she had hidden from him. Suddenly an even sharper thought stabbed through her—had he made the connection between K. T. Mays and Katy Mason? Outside in the balmy evening air, Katy waited for Tyler to slip the lasso around her neck and hang her out to dry.

"Do you want to tell me about the man who delivered the foreclosure notice from the bank?"

No. She really didn't, but she knew she would have to or walk away from a place she already loved. She took a seat on a deco metal glider. *Anything to kill time.* She'd lied about her last name, but she didn't want to lie about anything else.

"He and I dated for a while. It didn't end well, and I just didn't want to face him."

"Then you are familiar with the bank where he works?" Tyler's voice carried a note of coldness. Katy felt it crawl down her spine.

"I know he works for the savings and loan in Cantor." That was the truth. No lie there.

Please don't let him ask anything else about Jeremy or the bank.

"If it ended badly, I guess that means you can't put in a good word for us with this Mays fellow at the bank."

"Not very likely. As a matter of fact, if the chance arises, I wouldn't even mention my name." Katy smiled, but knew it wasn't convincing.

"According to the foreclosure notice, we have to pay the loan in full or vacate the premises. I've only been here a week. Just enough time to realize exactly how deep in trouble the ranch really is. Most of my money is tied up in investments. One of those has gone seriously south. I don't have the funds readily available to pay off the loan. I'm using the small amount I had left in my savings just to keep our head above water."

Katy wanted to ask what that bad investment was, but knew it wasn't the time for that. Although Tyler was right there in front of her, the shadows in his eyes plainly showed his mind was a million miles away. She certainly didn't want to delve into his private life or his thoughts, mainly because that would lead to questions about her. At that moment, she didn't want to think about any part of the life she'd turned her back on that very morning.

They sat quietly in the dusk and watched it rapidly turn to darkness. Lights, which she assumed were on automatic timers, began to click on, flooding the beautifully arranged flower beds flanking the main walkway and entire length of the front porch.

Katy moved to the railing and looked down at a row of blue hydrangeas. "The flowers are beautiful," she said, then noticed weeds sprouting throughout the beds.

"Those are Uncle Frank's pride. He always had good luck with gardening. Wait until you see his rose bushes behind the house. He's won blue ribbons at the county fair, but since he can't take care of them now, the weeds are taking over. I'm not sure if I'll be able to keep them alive."

Katy loved working with the soil. Even though her parents had a lawn service to cut the grass and trim the hedges, the flowers were a different story. She'd delighted in helping her mother in the lush gardens scattered over the property surrounding their house just on the outskirts of Cantor. However, wearing a wide-brim, floppy hat to keep the sun from sprouting freckles on her delicate skin was always a bone of contention between her and her mother. Katy loved the warm sun on her skin and usually defied her mom by wearing her hat dangling from drawstrings and hanging at the back of her neck.

Tyler leaned his head against the back of the bentwood rocker he'd been moving gently for the past five minutes. Since his eyes were closed, Katy stole the moment to study his carved features bathed in the shadowy light cast from the garden. Fatigue hardened the soft lines she'd noticed earlier in the day. His day's growth of beard lent to his weary, yet handsome looks. As she studied his full lips, her tongue automatically licked her own.

Her gaze slipped lower to his well-defined chest muscles and his trim waist. A very slight movement at the corners of his mouth startled Katy. Her gaze snapped to his eyes, opened and staring at her. They amped her heart's rhythm and kept her from looking away. If truth be told, she didn't want to. She wanted to understand the new look of concern in her boss's eyes.

"I'm sorry. Here I've been going on and on about the problems the ranch is facing, and never once have I given thought to your part in all this." Tyler's voice carried all the compassion and caring she'd seen in the depth of his gaze.

Her part? Oh, no, here it comes.

Katy's stomach twitched. Her heart stopped while she waited for Tyler to fire her for the part she had in trying to take the ranch away from Frank. Had he found out her true identity? She started to ask what he was referring to, but Tyler quickly continued.

"I'm sorry to have put you in this position. When I hired you this morning, I felt confident I could get an extension on the loan, and then I would need your help to keep everything running like the full facility dude ranch we have presented ourselves to be.

"I wish I could promise you things are going to work out, and you'll have a job for as long as you like, but right now, all I can promise is maybe three weeks. That could end up being nothing more than long hours of packing years of collections and memories Uncle Frank and my whole family, for that matter, have gathered."

Tyler rose. "My mother always says that it's hard to think clearly in the darkness. Therefore, you should turn anything that takes heavy thinking over to your subconscious mind and sleep on it. The light of day will be brighter and allow you to see the problems more clearly. That is what I intend to do for tonight. Maybe you should do that, too." He moved to the screen door and opened it for Katy. "I'll meet you in the office at eight, but if you aren't here, I'll know you've moved on, and I'll completely understand." His forced smile tugged at Katy's heart, but the gentleness reflected in his eyes sent her stomach plummeting.

Struggling to hide her overwhelming reaction to her new boss's scrutiny, she pushed away from the porch railing and made a straight line for the door.

"Thank you for your honesty." Katy spoke with as level a tone as she could manage and then escaped to her assigned room at the end of the hallway.

Tyler watched Katy's rapid retreat. And he was sure that by morning she would be out of his life. A pang of disappointment lay in the pit of his stomach. For the past few weeks he'd been dodging painful jabs to his heart and his ego, leaving his mind in a vulnerable state. Surely that was the reason the thought of Katy leaving left him saddened.

He'd recently been betrayed by the woman he thought loved him. There were many rungs of disillusionment that came with his fall down that ladder. He and Beth had been together *all* the time. They worked at the same company, lived together in a New York apartment, had been planning their wedding together, and Tyler had felt sure they were in love . . . together.

But sadly that all crumpled when he discovered his beloved Beth had hacked into his computer and stolen an advertising ad he'd spent weeks putting together for a mega deal with a computer company. The deal would have given him a large bonus and garnered him accolades that would have won him many more accounts for a long time to come.

Instead, Beth had put her name on it and turned it in as her own. He understood she'd recently been put on probation for not acquiring her own accounts, but Tyler never dreamed she would stoop so low as to steal from him. But she did.

She pleaded with him to keep the secret between them, but until that moment, he'd not seen her conniving side. Whether it was the act she'd committed or his naiveté that appalled him, it didn't matter. He couldn't overlook it. So he put his wounded pride aside and told their boss the truth.

Then the next sucker punch hit him even harder. Connor Fleming, CEO of Fleming Advertising Agency, told Tyler he believed his accusations were merely a case of sour grapes. In Fleming's eyes, Tyler had been bested by his fiancée, thereby doing major damage to his ego. His boss suggested Tyler take a little time off and get over it. His boss reminded him that he seldom ever took time off, and now would be a good time to get out of the city for a few days and then come back the following week rested and ready for a fresh start.

Tyler took that time off, but didn't leave town. He spent his time packing some of his stuff up in the apartment he and Beth had shared and then moved into a nice hotel where he spent the next few days trying to decide if he wanted to go back to work or try his hand somewhere else. But where?

Shortly before he was to return to work, the answer to that *where* question plopped into his lap. Uncle Frank needed his help. Tyler requested an extended leave of absence from the ad agency and jumped at the chance to go back to his favorite place in the world. The Dixie Rooster Ranch in Georgia. It couldn't have come at a better time, and, for Tyler, nothing could have been sweeter.

But little did he know the storm his cousin Sid had left behind struck the family ranch with gale force winds. Tyler wasn't sure he could ride out the bad weather, but he had a feeling it would be a lot more pleasant with Katy at his side.

THE SUN PEEKED through a slit in the curtains and slashed bright light across Tyler's face. He pulled the bed sheet over his head, but a second later threw it aside and scrambled to a sitting position. The clock couldn't be right. Seven fifteen.

In the distance, he heard hammering, which told him the crew he was supposed to meet at seven had started working without him. Torn about the uncertainty of the ranch, which had become even more precarious since he'd actually been handed the foreclosure notice, Tyler thought it better to let them continue on just in case he managed to find a soft spot in old man Mays' heart.

As fast as he could move, he slipped into a pair of jeans he'd borrowed from his uncle. He pulled on a chambray shirt and tried desperately to suck in his gut and force the snap at his waistband to close. Jamming his feet into his boots, he finger-combed his hair.

Usually by seven thirty he had prepared breakfast for Uncle Frank and himself. Cold cereal would have to be on the menu this morning. He touched the door knob, but drew back as if it had burned him.

Katy.

Would she be waiting for him, or would she have called her friend to come and pick her up? He couldn't blame her. She must think him a nutcase to give her a job and then a few hours later let her know that he was sorry for doing that.

Again, he grasped the knob, turned it, and walked out into the hall. He glanced first to his left. Katy's bedroom door stood open. He walked to it and saw her bed perfectly made as if it had never been slept in. There were no signs of her or her belongings. He dismissed the empty feeling inside him and went to the kitchen.

Uncle Frank sat at the table drinking coffee and reading an old issue of a *Farm and Ranch* magazine.

"Is cold cereal okay this morning? I'm running a little late." Tyler grabbed a box of shredded wheat from the top of the refrigerator.

Uncle Frank toasted his nephew with his coffee mug. "Just top me off with hot coffee, and I am good to go."

"So you don't want any breakfast this morning? What about your insistence that all ranch hands eat breakfast?" Tyler took a closer look at the elderly man to see if he might be under the weather, but Frank smiled.

"Your new assistant fixed me a delicious plate of scrambled eggs with cheese." He rubbed his belly in a small circular motion. "Best I've ever eaten."

So, before she made her great escape, Katy had seen to Uncle Frank's needs. Tyler mulled that thought around in his head. "Wish I'd gotten up in time for that."

"Check in there." Frank pointed at the white microwave setting on the countertop.

Tyler punched the button and then peeked inside the appliance. Sure enough, he found a plate of scrambled eggs topped with shredded cheese and two slices of buttered toast. He closed the door and set the timer. While he waited for it to ding, he poured himself a cup of coffee.

"Did Katy say anything before she left?"

"Yeah, something about bad weeds choking everything."

Ugh. Until that moment Tyler had only thought of Sidney as a bad weed, but did Katy think Tyler was also one? He assured himself he had no intention of hiring her only to pull the employment rug from under her a few hours later. He just didn't realize he may not be able to save the ranch, but the pipsqueak from the bank had made it appear to be pretty much a done deal. In all good conscience he couldn't expect Katy to stay with no future beyond the next few weeks.

Tyler ate his breakfast and finished his cup of coffee. "Do you want me to help you get situated somewhere so you can be comfortable?"

"Sure, how about putting me on top of the third bunkhouse and let me patch the roof. Now that's where I'd be most comfortable." Frank's eyes twinkled. His mouth sported the devilish grin that always warmed Tyler's heart. It was exactly like his dad's. That was about all he could vividly remember about him.

"Well, we both know that's not happening."

"Okay, help me roll out to the front porch. I can at least watch the facelift the ranch is getting, even if it is from afar."

Even if, in the end, we lose the whole place.

Tyler pushed aside his negative predictions and hurried to get behind his uncle's wheelchair in hopes of hiding the disappointment that surely scowled across his face. No need to further add to Frank's burdens. Tyler's ego was also taking a beating. He'd arrived at the ranch filled with smug confidence that he had the business sense it would take to dig the ranch out of the hole Sidney had put it in. It didn't take long for Tyler to realize things had been let go far too long for him to wave a magic wand and fix it for Uncle Frank.

When they got to the front of the house, the door leading to the porch was already open. Frank used his broken leg, which always remained elevated, to push on the screen door. Tyler got him settled in a place with a perfect view of the renovations going on directly across the driveway from the main house. He stepped around the chair to face his uncle, then locked the wheel just in case it decided to roll away. He certainly didn't need any more disasters to deal with.

Suddenly, behind him, Tyler heard rustling in the flowerbed in front of the porch. He hurried to the banister and looked down to see what was rooting among the hydrangeas.

Tyler looked down into Katy's twinkling brown eyes.

Chapter 5

"GOOD MORNING." Katy rose from her kneeling position in the flowerbed and dusted the dirt from her knees. "Did you find your breakfast in the microwave?"

Dumbstruck, Tyler finally managed to get completely formed words to come out of his mouth. "Ah, yes. Thank you."

"You're more than welcome." She pulled a pair of oversized, worn gloves from her hands and slapped them together to knock off any loose dirt. After glancing at her watch, she walked around to the steps and made her way up onto the porch.

Katy flashed Frank a genuinely beautiful smile. Tyler noticed it lost none of its sincerity when she looked at him. The warm excitement he'd experienced yesterday every time he'd looked at her flooded back with a force he wasn't sure he could handle. He stiffened his spine and held out his hand to take the gloves from her.

"What are you doing here so early?" Tyler discarded the gloves onto a nearby work bench and then opened the screen door for Katy.

"Since I don't have a job waiting for me anywhere else, why not stay here? The clean country air certainly can't do me any harm. And I'm hoping I might get a chance to ride one of the horses sometime."

Her genuinely happy laugh wrapped around Tyler's heart. He'd certainly taken a quick interest in his new assistant.

He hoped he wasn't shoving himself in harm's way. One broken heart a year was all he could stand.

"I'm going to clean up, and then I'll be ready to start in the office. Just give me a few minutes." Katy walked toward her room, but stopped quickly and spun to catch Tyler watching her.

Knowing it was fruitless to try to hide it, he just waited for her to speak and for the heat to leave his face.

"You seemed surprised that I didn't leave," Katy said. "Did you want me to?"

Startled by the question, Tyler paused for a few seconds and then shook his head. "No, I didn't. And for the record, I'm glad you stayed."

"Good. Tomorrow morning I'll tackle the rose garden in the backyard."

Long after Katy had closed the door, Tyler continued to stare at it. What was that strange feeling swirling inside him with the force of a tornado? Surely it wasn't caused by his new assistant whose eyes showed more kindness in one smile than he'd ever seen in any other woman. Especially Beth's.

WHILE TYLER WAITED in the office for Katy to join him, he re-read the foreclosure notice one more time, hoping to find a shred of hope for getting an extension. Of course, no legalese fairy had mysteriously crept into the office in the middle of the night and added any loopholes.

The best Tyler could hope to do would be to appeal to Mr. Mays' sense of loyalty to the business community of the township of Cantor and surrounding areas. Tyler couldn't think of a better time to call Mays and make an appointment to meet with him later in the afternoon. His hand barely touched the black desktop telephone. It rang. The caller ID showed Dr. Marlowe's number.

Tyler lifted the receiver and settled back in the chair. "Dixie Rooster Ranch."

"Frank Davis, please," a pleasant female voice eased its way to Tyler's ear and settled some of his irritation.

"This is his nephew. He's outside. May I help you?"

"Well, maybe. Mr. Davis has an appointment this morning in our Augusta office. Dr. Marlowe wants to remind him to bring all his medication."

"Oh, I didn't know about the appointment. What time is it?"

"Eleven thirty."

"Okay, I'll get him there."

So much for going to Cantor to talk to Mays. The trip to Augusta would take the major part of the day. He'd also planned to pick up a few groceries. Their larder, as Aunt Hilda used to call it, was pretty near empty. That thought lightened his heart and made him smile. Uncle Frank always said she was a *pistol,* and most of the time that's what he called her. Nothing in the world had ever been as plain to Tyler as his aunt and uncle's love for each other. When Aunt Hilda died, she took a large part of Uncle Frank's soul with her.

And, if the truth be told, she took part of Tyler's, too. He hadn't come back since she died. Now he regretted that and knew he'd done Uncle Frank an injustice. He should have come back to the ranch periodically, but over the last six years he found it easier to use work as an excuse than to have to face the heartache of his aunt's absence, Uncle Frank's sorrow, and leaving the ranch at the end of the visit.

Even now, Tyler knew he'd eventually have to go back to New York, and the homesickness he'd take with him would be hard to endure.

Katy appeared in the doorway. "I'm ready if you are."

Tyler rose and walked around the desk. "I just found out Uncle Frank has a doctor's appointment in Augusta in a couple of hours."

"Would you like me to take him?"

"I'm a little worried about Old Blue making that long trip. I'd better go just in case the old truck decides to act up. I'd planned to go to the bank this morning and buy groceries, but now I'll be going in the opposite direction. I can still go by the Bi-Lo Supermarket on the way home to pick up some provisions. The men working on the bunkhouses don't need to be supervised. So, I'm not needed here for that. What I really need you to do is start sorting through all this old mail and bills and try to make some sense of this chaotic mess. I don't even know where to tell you to begin."

"Let me worry about that. Is there anything else you'd

like me to do while you're gone?"

"I'm not sure how long that will be. The work crew will leave by four o'clock." Tyler started for the door, but stopped short. "Yesterday you saw me get the feed for the two horses in the stable. If I'm not back by five, would you mind feeding them for me?"

"Sure. I can do that. If you think of anything else, you can always call me."

Tyler leaned against the door facing. "I feel guilty giving you this monotonous task and then deserting you on your first day."

"There's no need for that. I like working with numbers, debit, credits. I can do that all day and be perfectly happy." And she had been for a few years now. She'd loved everything about her job as vice president in charge of loans except for the foreclosure part. That wasn't for her, and a load had been lifted from her heart when she decided to never have to do that to anyone ever again.

"Well, anything to do with accounting has never been my strong suit. By the way, you mentioned you'd like to go for a horseback ride. If you want, feel free to saddle up either one of the two in the stable. The property is totally fenced, but if you happen to get turned around, just drop the reins, and the horse will come back here." Excitement pulsed through her veins. She couldn't wait to ride again.

"Thanks." Katy smiled wide. "I may do that later."

By the time Tyler and Frank had left, Katy had opened every piece of mail and sorted it into piles: bills, most of which were overdue, things needing immediate attention, and things she wasn't sure what to do with. Next she tackled the checkbook, which appeared to not have been balanced in at least five months. Even for Katy, who dealt with checks and balances all the time, she knew this would be a challenge.

She turned on a radio setting on the credenza behind her. Seal's perfectly balanced vocals filled the office with "Kiss From a Rose." Katy loved the way the romantic music flowed through her, bringing a peace inside her she didn't even know she had been missing.

For several years, she had moved through life executing the plan her parents had laid out for her. She'd accepted it. Now she could see how much of herself had been lost in their best laid plans. And, even with the threat of her newly found love, the Dixie Rooster Ranch, going down for the third time, she would enjoy the intense pleasure surrounding her heart for as long as possible.

BY THE TIME Katy finished sorting, filing, and cleaning away several inches of dust, it was two thirty in the afternoon. Tired muscles burned between her shoulder blades, but pride in her accomplishment eased most of the physical ache. She had a fully detailed report ready for Tyler when he returned. Granted, some of it wasn't good news, but at least now he would know where the ranch stood financially.

She went to the kitchen and fixed herself a tall glass of tea, sweet and cold. Outside on the wide-planked porch, distressed by time and weather, she watched three workmen repair the roof of bunkhouse number three. Even though the sun had already moved well into the western sky, its hot rays spilled across the porch, eliminating any hope of Katy finding shade there.

She pressed the cold glass to her forehead and enjoyed the cool sensation against her warm skin. Until she'd stepped out into the afternoon heat, she hadn't given much thought to the fact that the main house wasn't cooled by air conditioning. There really hadn't been many hot days yet in that part of Georgia. All the windows in the house had been opened since she'd arrived at the ranch, and so far the cross ventilation had done a more than sufficient job of keeping the house comfortable.

The hound dog came up the steps and strolled over to her. He sat by her feet. "You have a beautiful place to call home, George." Katy took a sip of tea and scratched behind the old dog's ear. He leaned into her touch, and she increased her efforts. "Feel good, boy?" He gave her a low moan. "I'll take that as a yes."

The telephone rang from inside the house. She hurried back into the office to answer it.

"Dixie Rooster Ranch."

There was a short pause, and Katy thought the caller must have hung up, but then she heard someone breathing.

"Hello?" Keeping the receiver to her ear, she walked around the desk and sat in the chair.

"Ah, yes." A woman was on the line. "I'd like to speak to Tyler, please."

"I'm sorry. He isn't in at the moment. May I help you?"

Katy heard a distinct huff of disgust from the other end of the line, then a crisp, "Who, exactly, are you?"

She flinched at the ill-mannered question. "My name is Katy. I'm Tyler's personal assistant. Would you like to leave a message for him?"

"Why does he need a personal assistant? Especially one who calls him Tyler. He has a job waiting for him here in New York."

The rude words bristled through Katy and brought her protective nature forward in a way she'd never experienced. "I'm sorry, but I think Tyler would be the person to answer your questions. I'd be glad to tell him you called if you care to leave your name and number." She had no idea she could be so curt. She was used to treating customers, right or wrong, with helpfulness and Southern politeness. This new sense of confidence made her almost giggle out loud.

"Tell Tyler that Beth called, and I'll be expecting to hear from him. He has my number."

"I'll be happy to—" The line went dead. "And a good day to you, too." Katy hung up the phone and stared at it thoughtfully. Her natural curiosity made her speculate as to the kind of connection Tyler could possibly have with the abrasive woman named Beth.

Katy felt like a mama bear protecting her cub, and it surprised her. She wasn't prepared for the jealousy that niggled inside her. She barely knew Tyler, yet she'd already felt a sliver of affection for him and his uncle.

She glanced at the clock. It was almost four o'clock, and the two men still had not returned to the ranch. Surely they would be along soon.

When Katy was prioritizing the documents and mail scattered on every available surface of the office, she had come across a thick, untidy notebook labeled *History of the Dixie Rooster Ranch*. The thought of learning about the beautiful place she now called home excited her. Of course, she was there to line up the financial part and not snoop into things that didn't pertain to her job. Although she had a feeling Tyler wouldn't object to her taking an in-depth look into the information inside the notebook, she would ask his permission first.

The phone rang again. Katy answered on the second ring. "Dixie Rooster Ranch." The words rolled gently across her tongue.

"Hi, it's Tyler." His deep, yet crisp voice settled over Katy. Again she thought of the contrast between his and the arrogant tone of Beth's voice. She couldn't imagine the two as a pair.

"Sorry we are running so late. They removed Uncle Frank's cast, then they had to x-ray his leg and put a new cast on. He has to come back in a month."

"What's the date and time of the appointment?" Katy asked.

There was a short pause from Tyler. "May twenty-fourth at eleven thirty."

She flipped the pages of the desktop calendar to that date and made a notation on the correct day. "Okay, it's on the calendar."

"Great."

Although it came as second nature to Katy, Tyler sounded truly surprised that she would think to do that.

"How are things going there?" Tyler asked.

The sound of a car starting drew Katy's attention. She rose then walked to the window facing the gravel driveway at the front of the house. "The work crew is leaving right now. I've done all I can really do until we sit down and look everything over. There are decisions to be made. I can make suggestions, but the ultimate decisions will be up to you . . . and Frank, I presume."

"Wow, you've done in a few hours what I couldn't do in the week that I've been back at the ranch. I'm impressed. Is there anything we can talk about over the phone? Uncle Frank is in the barber's chair. I have a few minutes before I head to the Bi-Lo grocery store, and then hopefully get back to the ranch."

Katy's stomach knotted. She had to give him the message from Beth, but for a few seconds, she actually considered tossing the message. In the end, right triumphed over just plain wrong.

"You have a message from a lady." Katy used the term only out of respect for Tyler.

"Did she leave her name?" Tyler asked.

"Yes. Her name is Beth, and she says you have her number."

A long moment of silence filled the conversation. "Oh, I have her *number* all right. I'll give her a call after we hang up." Tyler searched his mind to see if there was anything else he needed to speak to Katy about. He couldn't think of anything, "Have you had time to go for a ride?"

"No, not yet."

"I never thought to ask you if you can saddle a horse on your own, or if you would rather I be there with you."

I vote for you being here. Surely I didn't say that out loud.

"Oh, I can take care of getting the horse ready for a ride. I'm not sure I'm going to do that today. There is something else I'd like to do, if it is okay with you?"

"What is it?"

"While I was cleaning the desks off, I found a notebook that says it's the history of the ranch. I'd like to read some of it and learn more about the Dixie Rooster. I didn't want to look like I was snooping."

"You know, I didn't even know there was such a file, but of course it's okay for you to delve into it. After you're finished, I may go through it, too. It will probably be close to dinner time before we get back there. Uncle Frank wants to pick up Chinese on the way home. Will that be okay with you?"

"That'll be great. I love Chinese. Thanks for asking."

"Okay. We'll see you in a few of hours."

Tyler listened to Katy say goodbye and waited for her to hang up before he disconnected his cell phone. The things he and Uncle Frank had done since leaving earlier were important and had to be done, but Tyler's thoughts had drifted back to the ranch and, more specifically, to Katy several times during the day.

He blamed it on his over-active imagination. There was no way he could be feeling this strong attraction for a woman he'd met a day and a half ago. But the minute she answered his phone call and her voice, warm and gentle, settled over him, he knew for sure it wasn't anything he'd conjured in his mind. Katy Mason had reached inside him and latched onto his soul.

Tyler glanced through the barber shop window. Uncle Frank's silver hair had been cut, and the barber had leaned the chair back so he could give his patron a shave. Tyler figured it would be best to call Beth and get that out of the way. He had no idea what she could want with him. He'd made it perfectly clear he didn't want her calling him anymore. When he got back to New York, he would call her, and then they would make final arrangements for him to get his belongings out of the apartment they had shared for two years.

Thinking it might be something important, he dialed her number.

The phone only rang one time. "Tyler, sweetheart." Beth's voice doused him like a bucket of ice water. Obviously, she'd checked her caller ID.

Why hadn't he ever noticed the harsh tone laced with arrogance that came from the core of Beth's being? In his case, it wasn't that love was blind. It was that love was stupid.

"What do you want, Beth?" Tyler didn't try to hide the irritation weaving like wet wool through his own voice.

"Aren't you tired of playing this game? It's time for you to quit playing cowboy and come back to the big city where you belong. I love you. Please tell me you'll get on a plane and fly home tonight. I miss you. I told you I was sorry, and I meant it."

Even her attempt at being sweet had lost its power, and Tyler knew it would never affect him again.

"Beth, you and I are over. The only thing left for us to do is for me to get my personal stuff out of the apartment and both of us go our merry ways. I'll let you know when I'll be back in New York to do just that."

"Oh, Tyler, you're breaking my heart. Does this mean you want your ring back?"

Tyler held back the first words he wanted to say, which was *Hell yes.* He hadn't thought about that happening. If anything, he figured Beth would sell it and keep the money. What was the proper protocol for something like that? He had no idea, but he did know, if she gave it back, he would sell it and use the funds to make major headway on paying off the ranch.

"I gave the ring to you. What you do with it is your decision. I can only tell you that the day you stole my ad campaign for the Martin Brothers' new line of computers and then had the nerve to turn it into our boss as your own work, that ring no longer stood as a symbol of our love. It was an emblem of deceit. Wear it in good health."

Tyler disconnected the phone. Disappointment filled his heart. Not for the loss of Beth, but because her phone call had wiped away the euphoria Katy's call had given him.

AFTER SPEAKING with Tyler over the phone, Katy opened the notebook containing pages and pages of handwritten and typed historical facts from the beginning of the Dixie Rooster Ranch. All the pages were in no particular order, just randomly stuck in there.

A timeline found among the handwritten pages showed that Shep Davis had bought the two hundred and twenty-six acres in 1882. It also said that he bought it as a fifth wedding anniversary for his beautiful wife, Lynette, who fell in love with it while on a trip from Atlanta to Savannah.

"How romantic," Katy whispered to the quiet room. She drew in a deep breath and wondered what it would be like to be that loved. Of course, with that thought she wondered if she'd ever be that lucky.

Shep and Lynette Davis were Tyler's great-grandparents. From the small amount of time she'd been around him, she suspected he had a few of those passionate traits his great-grandfather had possessed.

Katy flipped through a few more pages. Someone had done a tremendous amount of work gathering info for the file. It would take her a while to read everything in there. As she started to close the notebook, she saw a map stuck in a back pocket. Upon looking at it, she discovered it was a plot map of the ranch at the time it was originally bought and surveyed.

She recognized the stream that flowed through the property. There was no bridge crossing the water, nor was there a main highway running along the front section of the land. Nor was there the long sweeping driveway lined with crepe myrtle trees leading to the large main house she was sitting in right then. She thought how interesting it would be to find out how it had evolved to the sprawling ranch it was today.

On the map, Katy saw the handwritten words *Lynette's New House* scratched next to an X. As close as Katy could tell, that was at the far end of the property, across the meadow and possibly in the wooded area which was visible from the right side of the porch of the present day ranch house.

She closed the book and placed it on the neat and clean credenza. Since Tyler wouldn't be back for a little while, and there was still plenty of sunlight left, she pulled the front door closed and set the plastic clock hands on the sign letting anyone know who might come along that she would be back at six o'clock.

Once in the stable, Katy saddled the horse named Shiloh. It had been at least two years since she'd been on a horse. Excitement rose inside her. At first she had voted against going out in the warm afternoon with no one else on the ranch, but now that she'd seen the original plot map, she had to find out if Lynette's house was still standing.

She led the horse through the pasture gate. With a little help from an overturned bucket, she climbed into the saddle and instantly welcomed the joy that always came once she was seated on the leather, raised to a level where she could look the world straight in the eyes and smile.

Katy held the reins lightly, allowing the horse to stroll at its own pace. Strangely, she headed in the direction of where Katy figured the old homestead would be. She didn't rush her. She relaxed and swayed with the slow cadence of the horse's gait.

Once they had reached a small rise at the back of the pasture, Katy saw about a dozen or so horses grazing in a lush, green field near the stream. The sight left her breathless, but what really took her breath away was even further across the field and toward the back end of the property. She nudged the horse into motion and raced across the pasture.

Chapter 6

KATY GAVE SHILOH, the chestnut mare, free rein to gallop across the pasture toward the woods that made up the back property of the Dixie Rooster Ranch. Just beyond the first row of trees and nestled beneath a canopy of kudzu, Katy saw a flat rock column. Convinced she'd found the cornerstone of the original house, her heartbeat quickened.

As soon as she slid from the horse's back, Shiloh went directly to a stand of fig trees. Their neglected branches sagged with ripened fruit, and a mat of fallen and rotted figs covered the ground. The unpleasant odor didn't bother Shiloh. She pulled the fresh ones from the weeping branches and happily chewed her way through a few before Katy relaxed enough to believe the horse would not take off for the stable, leaving her behind.

Katy ventured closer to the remains of the old house. Her first impression proved right. Four cornerstones made of stacked flat rock supported the warped boards of the old porch elevated a couple of feet off the ground. The façade of gray, weathered clapboards leaned slightly to the right. Two openings which once had held window glass now sagged with the appearance of sad eyes trying unsuccessfully to close. The building was tired and ready to lie down.

Other than the front of the house and the floor of the porch, it was impossible to tell how much of the two-story structure still stood. Kudzu had crept up and over the two tall chimneys, still standing after all these years. The strong vine had wrapped itself around the old house and would soon steal its soul.

When Katy was young, and she and her brother, Aidan, would visit their Grandmother Mays' old plantation home, the two kids would roam all over the massive piece of land and explore its hidden treasures including a few old buildings. If Katy closed her eyes and listened, she could still hear her grandma say, "Those out buildings belonged to my daddy. They survived a harsher time in history when the South was violated by . . . Yankees." She always whispered that last word.

Katy and Aidan weren't sure why that was funny, but it did make them laugh. Grandma Mays would eventually join them. Remembering her grandmother's laughter filled Katy with intense pleasure, something she called upon any time she needed to shove negative thoughts aside.

She studied the old house which marked the beginning of the Dixie Rooster Ranch property. She released a soft chuckle. Aidan would have loved seeing this. Katy had no doubt what he would have to say about this old place covered with greenery and vines.

"Oh, look, Katydid, that house is being devoured by a huge, green dinosaur."

A tear formed in the corner of her eye. She missed Aidan, and for the one thousandth time wished their father hadn't forced her brother from her life.

Katy glanced at her watch. She'd been away from the main house for quite a while. She had to get back. After looking around for something she could climb on to get onto the horse, she found a large block of stone that formed two steps. She recognized them as carriage steps from the old homestead. Reluctantly, Shiloh followed Katy's lead and then stood still so she could climb into the saddle. The horse needed no urging. She took a head-strong lead and galloped for the stable.

Katy couldn't contain the excitement bubbling inside her. Now that she'd seen the very core of the origin of the Dixie Rooster Ranch, she longed to read the historical facts documented in the notebook.

TYLER SKIDDED Old Blue to a stop on the gravel driveway, blocking the passage of a delivery truck. The driver of the Pools by Design vehicle got out.

"Hi, are you Sidney Davis?" he asked.

"No, I'm Tyler Davis. What can I help you with?" He couldn't imagine why the man was looking for his cousin.

The driver extended his hand, and Tyler shook it, all the while wondering, *what has Sid done now?*

"We couldn't find anyone when we got here, but we knew where it was to go. So, your hot tub is set up. The water and chemicals are in it, and the water is heating."

"What hot tub? We don't want a hot tub." Tyler scratched his head, which was beginning to throb. "You have to take it back."

"I'm sorry, Mr. Davis." The man's face flushed bright red. "This was a special order. It's not returnable."

Tyler clenched his jaws until they ached. By this time, Uncle Frank had made it out of the car. His new walking cast allowed him to move under his own power with the help of crutches.

He joined the two men. "What's going on, Ty?"

Surprised to see Uncle Frank, Tyler stepped toward him. "Here, let me help you into the house."

"Heck no. I feel like Free Willie." Frank moved around Tyler and to the hot tub man. "What's this all about?"

"Sidney Davis had me come out and design a special hot tub for the patio behind the rec room, next to the pool. I just put it into its place. Should be ready for use late tonight."

Tyler glanced at his uncle. "Did you know about this?"

"No. Sidney made all the decisions of what would be done to bring the ranch into a state of the art, highfalutin dude ranch. I couldn't make much sense out of things he was doing. Hildie and I ran a guest ranch for many years. We didn't need things like fancy pool tables, tennis courts, or hot tubs."

"Tennis courts!" Tyler nearly choked. "Don't tell me we are expecting a tennis court to be put in."

"I wouldn't be surprised. Sidney kept telling me I was too backwoods, and I needed to trust him. At some point I grew tired of arguing. So, I stupidly just oversaw the workers and let him do what he thought was best." Uncle Frank's soft, defeated tone constricted Tyler's throat and threatened to stop his breathing.

"His best might turn out to be the worst for my ranch." Deflated and with shoulders slumped, Frank managed to make it to the porch and up the steps with his new crutches. Tyler let him do it alone. He didn't want to rob his uncle of any more of his self-respect.

He returned to the problem at hand. "Okay, so how much do we owe you for the hot tub?" He sighed heavily, resigned to face it whatever the price.

"Nothing. Since it was special ordered, it had to be paid in full before we did anything. All we had to do today was deliver it and get it ready for use. That's done." He handed Tyler an invoice marked *Paid in Full.* With a sigh of relief that it wasn't yet another bill to add to the growing stack, he half-heartedly thanked the man and headed in the direction of the barn.

Tyler took another glance at the paper in his hand. "At least the bank will be getting a *highfalutin* ranch." He shook his head decisively. "One thing is for sure, they will bury me in that pasture before old man Mays gets a tennis court when he comes to claim his prize."

Tyler didn't usually show his anger, but, at the moment, he wasn't sure whose neck he'd like to have his hands around—the banker's or Sidney's. Since neither was present, he picked up an empty coffee can from the top of a feed barrel and threw it with all the frustration he had in him at the opening at the back of the stable.

The projectile missed Katy's head by inches. She and Shiloh stopped short. Tyler ran to them.

"Did it hit you?" Instinctively, he laid his hand on her head. She insisted she hadn't been hit. "I'm so sorry." He continued to touch the damp wisps of auburn hair framing her face. "Your hair is almost the color of Shiloh's coat."

Although Katy didn't shirk from his touch, for a moment, Tyler wondered if he had stepped over an employee/employer line. But her smile reassured him she wasn't put off by his forwardness and melted his anger and warmed his insides.

"You know what they say—chestnut mare, beware." Katy's gentle laugh rolled through Tyler, shoving his frustration with

Sidney aside and replacing it with an overwhelming desire to be close to Katy.

Reluctantly he fought the sensation and stepped aside to let her pass. "I'll consider myself forewarned," he said.

Katy led the horse into the stable. Tyler retrieved the coffee can from the ground just outside the barn and then went to help Katy remove Shiloh's tack and hang her saddle pad to dry. Together they gave her a quick brushing and then used the coffee can to scoop a mixture of sweet feed and oats into feed boxes for her and the other horse.

"Come on." Tyler hooked his thumb toward the house. "I have to get the groceries out of the truck." After a few steps, he called over his shoulder, "I've got our dinner. Got to get it inside."

"Good. I'm getting hungry." Katy caught up with him, and although she took two steps for every one of his, she stayed beside him.

From the truck's bed, Tyler pulled a medium-sized, white ice chest. "Would you mind grabbing the two bags out of the front seat?"

Katy got the groceries and then followed Tyler to the kitchen. Uncle Frank sat at the table sans his wheel chair, his crutches propped nearby.

"I'm starving," he said. "Where's that *moo goo gai pan*?"

"Just a sec." Tyler lifted several Chinese take-out boxes from the ice chest. Into a large bowl, he dipped a big scoop of white rice and then smothered it with a mixture of chicken, snow peas, and mushrooms swimming in a sauce. He stuck the bowl into the microwave. "Let me nuke that for a minute, and then you can chow down."

While Tyler tended to Frank, Katy removed the rest of the cold groceries from the cooler and put them into the refrigerator. Together, she and Tyler put away the dry goods. Each time their arms brushed or their hands touched, the contact sent a shock of heat rioting through her body to all the right places. Every time it happened, she'd been unprepared for it. Her breath hitched, and her stomach dropped until she thought she'd have to leave the room for fear of Tyler finding out how his touch affected her. It was unfamiliar, but not unpleasant. In fact, it was quite nice and different from anything she'd ever experienced with Jeremy.

To keep such thoughts at bay, Katy hurriedly fixed two bowls of the Chinese food just like Tyler had done for his uncle. Once it was heated, they joined Frank at the table.

"How was your first day of work, Miss Katy?" The elderly man spoke in a strong yet gentle tone.

Katy met Frank's gaze and immediately appreciated his thoughtfulness. "I think it went really well. I managed to organize a major part of the important papers and mail." She looked at Tyler. "Will we sit down together tomorrow and go over what I found and discuss actions that need to be taken?"

He'd just shoved a large bite of food into his mouth. While Katy waited for his answer, she wondered if Tyler would be the one making the decisions or would Frank.

"Yes, that's the plan. You and I will go over all of it, and if there's something I need to discuss with Uncle Frank, we'll call him in."

The elderly man nodded. "If at all possible, try not to let that happen. You might push me into a heart attack." His seriousness startled Katy. Her gaze danced from Frank to Tyler.

He shook his head. "He's kidding."

Katy released a heavy sigh. "Okay, you got me." She smiled at Frank. "You have to forgive me. I come from a long line of somber people. My brother and I were always in trouble for laughing at inappropriate times, so I tend to take things more seriously than I should."

"I'll try to remember that. How about if I raise my hand when I'm joking?" Frank stared at Katy and then wiggled his eyebrows.

A sound rumbled from deep inside her. She brought her hand to her mouth to stifle the giggle, but it did no good. Laughter filled the air, and, for the first time in a long time, Katy chuckled out loud. Frank and Tyler laughed, too. She reveled in the shared moment and tried not to relate it to her former home life. Even for the few fleeting moments, there was no comparison. She sensed its realism, and she liked it.

"Did you and Shiloh have a good ride this afternoon?" Tyler asked and then looked at Katy, appearing truly interested in her response.

"Yes, I did. I found an 1880's map of the Dixie Rooster Ranch. I rode out to where I thought the original homestead might be. There it was in all its vine-covered glory. It must have been a splendid house, back in the day."

"You know, I can't remember the last time I was out there." Frank took the last bite of his meal.

"Have you ever thought of having it listed with the Cantor Historical Society?" After seeing the remains of the old house, Katy had given this question a lot of thought.

"Yeah, the old bitty that has headed it for years tried to get us tangled up with them. Hildie didn't like her too much. The group wanted to tell us what we could and couldn't do on our own ranch. There would be people traipsing all over the place whenever they wanted to, and we would have to up our insurance to cover the liability." His wide smile told Katy there was more to this story. "Hildie told the high and mighty lady what she could do with her plaque, and believe me, I just cleaned the language up for you."

Katy joined the Davis men in a full round of belly laughter, and a wonderful feeling of belonging seeped into her soul.

Tyler gathered the bowls from the table and took them to the sink. When Katy started to rise to help him, he waved her off. "You sit here and keep the old man occupied."

"Hey, boy. This old man can take you any time . . . after I get my cast off, that is."

There was nothing Katy would enjoy more than delving into the history of the ranch. And she'd bet her newly-found independence that Frank had many interesting stories to tell.

"How did the Dixie Rooster Ranch get its name?" Katy took a sip of her cold, iced tea.

"Oh, that's a good one," Frank snorted. "My great grandfather Shep Davis was on a trip from Atlanta to Savannah with his new bride, Grandma Lynette. They passed by here, and she fell in love with the place. She wanted to give the spread what she thought was a French name—the Dixie *Chanticleer*. But when Grandpa Davis went to claim the two hundred twenty-five acres, neither he nor the gentleman in the land office knew how to spell *Chanticleer*. When asked what it meant, my grandfather said it's a rooster." Frank held out his hands with his palms up and shrugged. "And that's how the ranch got its name."

"Well, it's beautiful no matter which name it goes by, but if I had a vote, it would be *Chanticleer*."

"Why is that?" Tyler put the last of the dishes into the cabinet.

"This morning when I went out to work in the garden, it wasn't quite daylight yet, so I drank my coffee and watched the horizon. Orange and yellow streaked through the blue-black sky and reminded me of the colors of a beautiful rooster. I thought somewhere in this big world there was a rooster singing the sun awake. Within a few minutes, the sky turned to a bright, sunlit blue. Beautiful sight."

"I've watched that sunrise many times." Frank's voice sounded tired. "But I never thought of it like that."

"I wonder what your grandmother said about the name change," Katy asked.

"According to my mother, Grandma Lynette never accepted that. Until the day she died she called it the Dixie *Chanticleer*." Frank's smile mingled with a yawn.

Tyler sat at the table next to Katy. "You've had a long day, Uncle Frank."

"That I have, Tyler. Before I head off to bed, though, there is something I want to say."

For a moment, Katy wondered if what Frank wanted to say was private and she should leave the room, but neither the elderly man nor Tyler gave any sign they wanted to be alone.

Quickly, Frank continued. "I gotta tell ya, I don't know what I would do without you here sorting out the mess that Hildie's son made."

"Oh, so that's the way it is, huh?" Tyler shook his head

knowingly. "When he was hitting grand slams on the Little League field, he was *your* son. Now that he has caused you some pretty hefty grief, he's Aunt Hildie's son."

Frank's smile faded, replaced by an intense look of urgency. "Seriously, Ty." Frank's voice cracked a little. "I appreciate everything you are doing. And no matter how things turn out, I know you will have put your all into trying to save the ranch. I do thank you for that."

He pulled his crutches to him and then pushed himself onto his feet. The smile he tried to flash at his nephew was brief. The effort it took for him to become mobile displayed hard on his weathered face.

Katy admired the old man's courage and wondered if her father was ever in a position like Frank Davis was now, how would he handle his world being snatched from under him? How silly for Katy to have such a ridiculous thought. Her father would never be the underdog in any situation. And heaven help the person who tried to put him there.

Frank stood as tall as possible and rolled his shoulders. "I've broken wild horses for a full day and never felt as whipped as I do today. This old man is going to bed. Good night, Ty. Miss Katy."

"Good night," she replied and watched him maneuver his way out of the old farmhouse kitchen. Even with the threat of losing the ranch hanging over their heads, the Davis men created an atmosphere of a loving and caring family. And, for some strange reason, Katy could easily pretend she was part of that close circle.

When she was growing up, dinner around the Mays' family table usually consisted of Katy, her mother, and her brother. Her father almost always worked late. He usually didn't come in until she and her brother were already in bed. He contended that's what it had taken to provide for his family's many needs and wants, which he never let them forget. He never understood that the *wants* and *needs* he saw as essential to his family were not the ones they longed for.

It wasn't until she started working with her father that she found out he always left the bank before closing time. She would see his car in the parking lot of the Cantor Country Club.

A few years ago, Aidan had left home. His empty chair struck so much sadness in her heart that usually Katy opted to take her meals to her bedroom or out on the massive front porch. She'd do anything not to be reminded that their father didn't care enough to come home, and he'd dismissed Aidan from their lives with no signs of regretting his actions.

But most of all, she wanted to escape listening to her mother make excuses for the inexcusable things her father did. What she really wanted from her mother was to know why, in the name of everything that was holy, did she put up with her husband's verbal abuse?

Even as she thought it, Katy knew the answer. It was for the same reason she had jumped into Aidan's place. The last thing she wanted was to make her dad unhappy. She had striven to live her life just as it was designed by him, but in the end, she couldn't walk the narrow line Bill Mays laid down. She'd made the only choice left—to do what was best for her even if it meant she had severed all ties with her dad. Just as her brother had done.

Following their father's design was not for Aidan. He wanted to be a therapist helping children with special needs. To him, that was so much more rewarding than to work in the bank like their father had insisted he do. In the end, their father had given Aidan an ultimatum just like he had given Katy, and he chose what was best for him.

Aidan walked away that day leaving Katy to step into the big shoes their father had made for her brother. She'd tried, but failed miserably. The banking business was not for her any more than it had been for her brother. When it came down to it, her father had given her an ultimatum also—serve the foreclosure papers or find another job.

She had chosen the latter, and no matter how things turned out, she would be forever grateful for whatever time she had left on the ranch. Dixie Rooster or Dixie *Chanticleer.* It didn't matter. Neither name reflected the true beauty of the ranch. But through that day, as Katy had ridden through the fields, watched the horses graze, and had her first glimpse of the long-forgotten house which was as old as the Dixie Rooster Ranch itself, she knew she would cherish those memories and hoped to build more for a long time to come.

"Penny for your thoughts." Tyler pulled Katy from her reverie.

Flustered and not wanting to admit she was daydreaming of a future right there on the ranch, she scrambled to make up something. "Ah . . ."

Chapter 7

SITTING AT THE long, hardwood kitchen table, Katy had appeared lost in deep meditation. When Tyler offered a penny for her thoughts, she'd stuttered a moment, but gave no answer. Instantly, guilt washed through him.

"I'm sorry. That was an impolite question. I have no right to pry into your business."

"The question was fine. I guess I was a little embarrassed to be caught daydreaming."

All evening, Katy's cheeks had glowed with a sweet tinge of pink which Tyler presumed was from her ride in the sun. Now, that color had darkened to scarlet and had also deepened his desire to know what was going on in that pretty head.

"Last chance," Tyler teased. "I'd love to know what you were thinking that made you blush."

"Truthfully, I was reflecting on everything I'd done and seen today and filing those things into my memory for safe keeping."

"I'm glad you like it here. It's always been dear to my heart, but I like knowing someone other than family appreciates its beauty." The radiance of Katy's smile warmed Tyler's heart, and when he gazed into her eyes, a delightful sensation of wanting ran through him.

Tyler shoved that feeling aside and rose from the table. He had to put space between him and Katy. Although it didn't really matter what time it was, he glanced at his watch.

"It's been a long day. I'm going to lock up and go to bed." Tyler slid his chair back under the table. "Can I get you anything?"

"No, I'm fine." When Katy reached the door, she turned to face Tyler. "I'll be in the office by eight, if that suits you."

"Works for me. Night."

"Good night." Katy made the few steps into the hallway then turned right and into her bedroom.

Tyler exhaled a long breath. "What is wrong with you?" He hadn't meant to speak that out loud, but he did, and it helped him reel back in the invisible line from him to Katy. Right now, losing control of his heart and soul was not an option.

KATY HAD TURNED off the alarm clock an hour before it was set to go off. Excited to face her second day on the ranch, she dressed in the same clothes she had worn the day before. After she'd played in the dirt, weeding the garden, she would shower and dress in clean clothes. Besides, she had very few outfits suitable for the country. She definitely needed to get some jeans and blouses before too much longer.

Since it was still dark outside, Katy sat at the desk situated in the corner of her bedroom. Tyler had explained that Frank had made it for his wife from maple taken from the woods there on the ranch. Inside the drop-leaf she found stationery with the ranch logo, a beautiful, vividly-colored rooster.

Katy used a few pages to make a list of the things she wanted to check into and eventually pass on to Tyler as possible ways to pull the Dixie Rooster out of its descent into foreclosure. She also made her own to-do list, which included getting into town to buy some more clothes.

Also, she wanted to check her savings account. She hadn't brought her passbook with her, and she couldn't remember what the balance was. Not that she thought Tyler would accept any money from her, but maybe if he got close, her small amount might help bail them out of the foreclosure . . . at least a temporary measure.

For a fleeting moment, she wondered what her dad would say if her money kept him from getting his clutches on the ranch. Katy expected to feel some kind of satisfaction from that thought, but that wasn't to be. Shudders thundered through her, shaking her back to the world where Bill Mays struck fear in her heart.

She sucked in a fortifying breath and rose from the desk. "I'll face that angry bear when the time comes."

On her way to the flower gardens in the front yard, Katy stopped by the kitchen to fix coffee. There she found the pot almost full and steaming hot. Tyler or Frank must already be up. She poured her cup and added a dash of sweet cream and headed outside. The front door was opened. A sign that, despite it still being fairly dark outside, the day on the ranch had already started.

Katy went onto the porch and crossed to the railing. She sensed a presence behind her. Spinning around, she found Tyler sitting on the glider swing.

"Good morning." He raised his coffee mug.

"You're up early." Katy took a seat on a rocking chair which faced Tyler.

"I decided it's been too long since I've watched the sun rise above anything other than skyscrapers. You reminded me how beautiful it is above those distant hills." He slid over and patted the place next to him on the swing. "Sit here. You can't see it with your back to it."

Katy only hesitated a moment. She hoped she hadn't appeared too eager, but sitting next to Tyler and watching the sun come up would be a great way to start her day. In the serene quiet, with only the distant sound of the nearby creek rippling over its rocky bed, they watched the horizon come alive with an explosion of color that quickly melted away to make room for the clear blue sky.

With Tyler next to her, the display was even more beautiful than the day before. Katy's whole body came alive with desire, yet her heart told her the man next to her was in too much of a crisis mode for her to take a chance he was thinking clearly. And, in the back of her mind, she wondered what part Beth played in Tyler's future.

Quickly, Katy jumped to her feet. "I better get to work before the heat moves in. I'll work out here about an hour, and then I'll get showered and ready to meet you in the office by eight." She hurried down the porch steps and went to the flower bed at the far corner of the yard.

Katy's quick departure settled over Tyler, causing the air around him to rapidly change from pleasant warmth to a cool swirl of abandonment. He stared after her, baffled as to why he had to fight to keep from chasing after her and crushing her body to his.

Maybe the country air had stirred his animal instincts. Or, maybe there was such a thing as soul mates, and Katy Mason held the key to his happiness.

WHEN TYLER WENT to the kitchen to fix Frank's breakfast, he found his uncle eating a bowl of puffed rice. He'd managed to pour his own coffee and somehow get it to the table.

"You certainly are getting around well this morning. Is there anything I can get you?"

"Naw, I'm fine as fiddle dust. How are things going with you? Seems to me you and your new assistant are getting along famously. How's that working for ya?"

"I don't really know yet. Katy's taken on the job I gave her swiftly and with confidence. She acts like she has a handle on sorting things out. I'm about to find out how that's working for me."

"I really meant on a more personal level. The last time I saw you have those puppy-love eyes, you were giving your heart to your first grade teacher, Miss Gilbert, and along with that, all the peanut butter and jelly sandwiches she could ever eat."

"Aw, Miss Gilbert. She always smelled like cinnamon toast, and her shoes squeaked every time she took a step. Yes, I remember her fondly." And Tyler really did. She had been the person to break the news to him that his father had died. She'd held him while he cried, and he never forgot her kindness in a time when his whole family was struggling with the loss of a brother and a husband.

Looking back, Tyler knew he wasn't deliberately overlooked. Years later, in a heart to heart talk with his mom, he came to understand the depth of her loss and how she had to handle her own before she could help Tyler.

"I wonder where Miss Gilbert is now." He took his coffee mug from the counter and headed to the door.

"She married a judge from Augusta. He died several years ago. Wanna look her up and see if she still smells like cinnamon toast?" Frank chuckled in that way only he could.

Tyler shook his head and laughed all the way to the office at the front of the house. Katy waited there for him. He carried a straight-backed chair around to the backside of the desk. After placing it next to her, he sat down.

Katy reached for the first pile of papers. The top page was her hand-written notes of what needed to be questioned or what action needed to be taken. Tyler scanned the other four piles, each topped by a similar note.

The enormity of it all stunned him, but Katy remained unruffled and quickly explained things that he needed to know.

"I've divided this into two lists of utilities, wages, supplies, and major purchases bought for the ranch's renovations. The first column is what was paid out since the loan was taken out six months ago. The second is what has been paid since you arrived."

Tyler studied the long list of Sidney's extravagant purchases. The staggering amount of pay-out funds for those big-ticket items hit Tyler hard in the pit of his stomach. It appeared that his cousin had taken the major part of the loan he'd coerced Uncle Frank into taking out and spent almost all of it on things like thousands of dollars' worth of new tack and saddles and an upscale slate pool table with almost any accessory you could name.

Checking out the storage area over the recreation room and the three out buildings behind the main house quickly moved to the top of things Tyler had to do immediately. Heaven only knew what Sidney had bought and stored somewhere on the ranch. He would see what he possibly could return for a refund.

Katy gave Tyler time to absorb the news that no doubt shook him to his boots. Once she was sure he wasn't going to suffer a stroke, she handed him another sheet of paper and an envelope.

"Here is an estimate for a tennis court. It appears Sidney accepted the contract for installation and wrote a check for several thousands of dollars as a deposit."

"Please tell me you are kidding," Tyler begged.

"No, I'm not kidding, but there is a bright side to this situation."

"Ah, bright side. I could use one of those." He rubbed his hands together like a child waiting for an ice cream cone.

Katy leaned back in the chair and waited for him to look at what she'd handed him. "I didn't open it," she remarked, "but I have a feeling the deposit check and original contract is inside that envelope."

Tyler ripped into it. "You're right. So, this money is still in the bank. That's great."

Katy nodded. She couldn't find necessary IDs or passwords to access the ranch's bank account. The truth was, she'd called one of the tellers at her dad's bank. She and the new employee had formed an instant bond. Katy was sure she could trust her not to tell anyone she'd called. With her friend's help, she had determined there had been no withdrawals since Sidney had cashed the final check he'd written to himself. But she certainly couldn't tell Tyler she had that kind of connection to access his accounts.

"According to the date on the last statement, a new one should arrive in the mail in the next day or two. We can verify the true balance as soon as it comes in." She hoped that would keep him from asking anymore questions in that vein.

Tyler started to say something, but held back. Katy took advantage of that and moved to another pile of papers. "I found an inventory of the ranch's assets. Most of the new stuff Sid had bought had not been added to the list. I added them as best I could, and I thought we should do an inventory as soon as possible, so you can get an idea of assets that can possibly be liquidated quickly."

"Wow, you really understand how this ranch operates. These are things I would never have thought of."

"I don't really understand the workings of a ranch. I do, however, understand the workings of a business. Assets and liabilities are the same no matter what the business is."

"That is certainly true. Is there anything else that needs my attention immediately?" Tyler carried his chair back to the front of the desk.

"No, I still have a few files to go through, but I think all the surprises have worked their way to the surface."

"Good." Tyler leaned against the door facing. "I've decided not to approach Mays at the bank until I have a substantial amount of the outstanding money in my hand. I'm hoping it might entice him to give us a little more time if we show him we are seriously trying to pay off the loan. Do you have any thoughts about that?"

Katy leaned back in her chair and crossed her arms. She tapped her finger on her forearm. She had plenty of thoughts on that, but she didn't dare express them to Tyler. Her dad wanted that property in the worse way. She knew in her heart he would settle for nothing less than the full amount.

A statement Jeremy always used, which cut sharply into Katy's last nerve on a daily basis, flashed through her thoughts. *Don't get your hopes up.*

Well, why not? How can you go through life never getting your hopes up or setting a goal for something? She certainly wasn't going to be the one to smash Tyler's hopes.

"Having most of the money is a good goal," she lied and forced a smile. "Can't hurt. Might help. Either way, it's definitely worth a shot."

Relief brightened Tyler's face. Immediately a painful pressure grew in Katy's chest. Her conscience swayed a little, urging her to tell him the truth, but in the end, she let it go.

"This may sound crazy"—Tyler sat in the chair across the desk from Katy—"but I'm thinking about running some ads in different places to try to bring in more business. If we can gather a few major reservations that will help get money for the loan."

"I know this is none of my business, but won't it take a considerable amount of funds to pay for advertisements? Do you want to throw good money after bad?"

"As far as the design, that's what I've been doing since I graduated from college, and I'm good at it. That won't cost anything other than my time. And I have favors owed to me from inside the advertising business." Tyler's gaze drifted past Katy and fixed on something behind her.

She wanted to turn to see what he was looking at, but instead continued to stare at his handsome profile etched with a secret expression. What was he thinking? Even the twitch at the corners of his mouth reminded Katy of her brother's smirk when he knew something Katy didn't. Dealing with Aidan for all those years had taught her to sit back and wait. He'd tell her in his own time.

Tyler didn't take long to tell Katy what was on his mind. "Beth is the perfect person for this job. She owes me big time."

Chapter 8

TYLER STOOD INSIDE the office of the Dixie Rooster Ranch. Katy sat behind the desk, trying to absorb the meaning of his last statement. With his declaration that he would ask Beth to do a job for him and that she owed him big time, Katy sank back in her chair. Apparently, he still had some connection to the woman who had been so rude to Katy. An odd twinge of jealousy slithered through her.

Miffed at herself for even feeling the slightest bit of possessiveness, she shut the top desk drawer a little harder than she should have. Her gaze snapped to Tyler, but apparently he was still thinking of Beth and hadn't noticed Katy's unwarranted reaction to his mentioning the snooty New York woman.

What exactly was their relationship? Better yet, why did Katy think she had the right to feel possessive of Tyler or even know anything about his personal association with the woman? Evidently she needed to remind herself that less than seventy-two hours ago, she was engaged to Jeremy. A reality check was in order for Katlyn Mays or Katy Mason or whatever she was calling herself that day.

She hated to break her boss's trance, but she didn't want to sit idly by when she was sure there were many things she could be doing that would be attached to her job. It would do her good to remember she was Tyler's assistant, not his love interest or paramour or even his keeper.

"What would you like me to do next?" She rose and then placed her open palms against the desk.

"I want to get busy working up an ad for the ranch. I should be able to do it by late this afternoon and still have time to send it over the Internet to Beth."

Katy thought she saw sparks of excitement shoot from

Tyler's eyes. Was that for the advertisement he would work on or for the pleasure of working with Her Highness Beth? Katy needed something to counter balance her lustful thoughts and jealous notions. Remembering a silly thing she'd learned in one of her psychology classes, she pulled a thick rubber band from the desk caddy and slipped it onto her wrist.

Since Tyler eyed her with suspicion, she chose not to pull it back and let it sting her flesh, which she had learned from her professor was a method used to break a habit or to derail derogatory thoughts.

"I'm sure I could look around and find something to do, but is there any place in particular you would like me to start?" As his beautiful blue-eyed gaze appeared to rake over her face, heat rose from her body, sending a quiver down her spine. Oh, why did he have to look at her that way? See, this was exactly why she'd become so possessive of him. Katy put her hands behind her back and then stretched and released the rubber band. It snapped loudly and painfully against her skin, hurting like a bee sting, but she pretended she hadn't heard it.

"You mentioned yesterday needing to do an inventory of the storage area and the attic over the rec room. Would you like me to start working on that?"

"Ah, no. I have a big favor to ask of you."

Katy was taken aback by Tyler's apologetic tone. She couldn't even begin to imagine what he wanted her to do, but whatever it was, she knew she would do her best to assist him. After all, wasn't that her job?

"I'll try," she said.

"The foreman overseeing the restoration here somehow underestimated the amount of shingles he needs for the roofing job. Cole Lewis at the building supply place in Cantor has a bundle, but he can't spare anyone to deliver it out here. Would you mind driving Old Blue to pick up the shingles? Cole will load them for you." Tyler pulled his wallet from his back pocket, opened it, and then handed her a fifty-dollar bill. "I wasn't sure about the reliability of the old truck, but after I drove it to Augusta yesterday, I'm pretty sure it will make it to Cantor and back. Would you mind?"

Katy took the money and shook her head. "No, I'd be glad to do it." This lying thing was getting easier and easier, because there was nothing she wanted to do less than go into town where she was sure to be spotted by someone. But, of course she would do it. If someone saw her and started questioning her about where she's been, she would just have to lie her way through it. She appeared to have developed a propensity for that.

As Tyler left the office, Katy watched his rear with intense interest. She pulled her deterrent rubber band out and released it with a loud snap.

"Ugh." The groan slipped past her lips before she could capture it.

Tyler spun to face her. "You okay?"

"Oh, sure. I accidently stung myself with this rubber band." She certainly wasn't about to tell Tyler that she'd been moved to drastic measures to keep from thinking of him as anything other than her boss.

AS TYLER WALKED Katy to the old truck and started to pull open the door for her, he took a close look at the ranch's logo displayed on Old Blue's side. The once vibrant picture with the beautiful colors of a boastful rooster had mutated into a faded, sad-looking turkey with missing tail feathers. An odd sensation charged through him. He turned to Katy.

"In all that stuff you went through yesterday, did you happen to see any paperwork on a new vehicle?"

"Yes, I did. The title was in a stack of unopened mail. That is one of my questions. Where is the 2012 Ford F250? That can definitely be liquidated."

"I wish I knew. I'll check the out buildings, but my guess is Sid took it. Later on today we can go through the rest of those files you did yesterday." Tyler opened the door, and Katy climbed into the truck. "I need to get all the surprises over with before I have a stroke."

She chuckled. "There are only a couple of things we haven't

talked about yet. We can take care of that later in the afternoon. Good luck on your ad."

After getting off to a jerky start, Old Blue coughed one time hard, and then it and Katy disappeared out of Tyler's sight. He lifted his gaze to the mostly-blue sky. Only one dark cloud hung there. He certainly hoped the rain held out until Katy got back. He didn't know if the truck had windshield wipers.

Back inside the main house, Tyler found Uncle Frank enjoying his favorite pastime—watching television through closed eyelids. His uncle had a special place in Tyler's heart. Sometimes that spot was so soft it brought him pain. After his father died, Frank had quickly moved from uncle to the best father figure anyone could ever ask for. Every bit of Tyler's knowledge of living in the South and working on a ranch came from his uncle.

Tyler had no problem answering the question that always came on the first day back to school. *What had he done on his summer vacation?* Thrilled to report, he'd tell his class how he'd spent the last three months riding, feeding, and currying horses. But, for some reason, he never reported to his classmates the best part of his time spent on the ranch. Tyler followed Uncle Frank around, wanting so much to learn everything he could from him. After all, he was the smartest man Tyler knew.

The one constant that never changed was Sid the Snake's masterful disappearance act when there was work to be done. Tyler shook his head. Even in adulthood, his cousin resorted to that approach to life. Just pick up and take off. Anger jabbed Tyler's stomach. Only this time, Sid had put his father and the ranch in harm's way. Tyler didn't plan on letting this stunt go unpunished.

"You're concentrating on something mighty hard, boy." Frank shifted his slight body and sat a little straighter. "You've only been here a short time, but your frown lines have deepened three-fold."

"Oh, well, at least I have a mission in life." He didn't dare tell Uncle Frank that his mission was to do bodily harm to his one and only son. Tyler chuckled silently. Even though he was only kidding, it did bring him a small amount of pleasure to imagine the wrath he'd like to rain down upon his cousin.

"Do you need anything, Uncle Frank? I have to get to work."

"I can get anything I need all by myself thanks to these here crutches. 'Preciate it."

Tyler went to the office. Shortly after he'd arrived at the ranch, he'd discovered the latest model computer, all powered up with wireless Internet. Sid strikes again. Tyler had used it to access his email account, but once he realized most of the emails were from the last person he wanted to hear from, he deleted all of Beth's posts and hadn't returned to the computer since.

Now, he needed to access some of his online graphic sites, and a brand-new computer with fast-access Internet would come in very handy.

"Thanks, Sid," Tyler mumbled begrudgingly under his breath.

KATLYN MAYS OF Cantor, Georgia, did something she'd never dreamed she would have to do. She parked the blue pickup with the faded Dixie Rooster Ranch logo on its doors at Friendship Park on the edge of town. Then she stealthily made her way by foot toward her parents' house on Ronstadt Street, being careful not to make eye contact with anyone. She'd even been forced to step into a store entrance to avoid coming face to face with Patience Everson, Jeremy's mother.

Katy had once been guilty of sneaking *out* of her home, but never into it. She prayed all the way there that when she arrived at the house where she'd grown up, her mother's car would be gone.

Katy needed money, and when she'd originally left home, she'd neglected to take her checkbook. Now she needed it and also wanted her savings passbook. Today wasn't one of her mother's regularly scheduled club meetings or card playing days. So, the chances of her not being at home were slim.

Thankfully, when Katy arrived, her mother's Cadillac was

not in the driveway. She used her key to slip through a side door and up the back stairway. It didn't take but a second to get what she'd come after. She stuffed them into her purse and started to leave, but a reflection in the mirror above her dresser caught her attention. Seeing the miniature white tea set her mother had given her when she was eight caused Katy's heart to ache and forced her to take one more look at her old room.

At age twenty-eight, why had she not realized how child-like her room was? *She'd* grown up. Her surroundings had not. She compared the room to the one she had at the ranch. Hilda Davis had beautiful, decorative tastes, one that fit Katy's style, but maybe that room needed a little of Katy's own touch. She wrapped the tea set in a crochet scarf and put it into her purse with her bank books.

One last sweeping glance, and then she had to get out of there. On her dresser lay the engagement ring Jeremy had given her. Guilt nearly consumed her. She picked up the expensive token of Jeremy's love, or as she had learned from her last conversation with him, his deposit on a secure future. Katy slipped the ring into her pocket. Later, when she had time to think clearly, she would figure out the best way to return it to him.

Jeremy had given it to her, but she didn't want it around as a reminder. He wasn't the only one who had made their commitment for the wrong reason. She was just as guilty. She'd deceived Jeremy, and herself in the process, into believing she loved him. That was so wrong, and that was something she needed to make right as soon as possible.

At the bottom of the stairs, Katy had taken only a few steps into the hallway when someone spoke behind her.

"What are you doing here, Katlyn?" Her mother's voice stopped her.

Katy spun to find her mother with no makeup, her hair awry, and wearing a day dress normally reserved for yard work. She knew instantly that her mother had been home all the time.

"Where's your car?" Katy stood frozen where she'd stopped.

"It's at Buddy's getting a tune up. Does that mean that if it had been in the driveway, you wouldn't have come in?" Sadness laced her mother's soft voice and landed hard in Katy's chest.

"No, of course not. I would have come in."

Liar. Liar. Pants on fire.

"I don't know for sure, Mom. Sorry. I needed my bank books, and I picked up my engagement ring so I can return it to Jeremy." Katy knew those words would hurt her mom deeply.

"So you've said goodbye to me, to your father, and to the man you love. How can you do that?"

She wasn't as shocked at her mother's question as she might have been. She wasn't sure how to justify it all to her mother, so she wouldn't try. The truth was what needed to be said at that moment.

"Sadly, I don't think I ever loved Jeremy. Where he is concerned, it's the right thing to do. As for you, it's Daddy I'm trying to get away from. I hate the banking business, and by walking out on the bank, I knew it meant also leaving Dad behind. Just like Aidan did." Katy waited a moment for her mother to absorb all that. Katy had learned early on to never back talk or argue with anything her mother said. The few times she had rebelled against her mother's wishes, Mom had gone directly to Katy's dad, and he'd gladly reminded his daughter which side her bread was buttered on.

After a few incidents like that, Katy found it easier to just do what was expected of her and not to raise a fuss, no matter how small. Until recently, not voicing an objection had become a natural part of her chemistry. Now was the time to take her soul back.

"I have to get my life grounded. And that means not living with Dad's number one rule that everything has to be done his way or else. I'm sorry if I hurt you. I just want to make my own plans for my future. Is that really so wrong?"

Tears welled in her mother's eyes. "I want nothing more than for you to be happy, but I sincerely hope you don't push me aside while you are making your new life. I don't want that to happen."

Katy fought to keep her tears from falling. "It won't, Mama, I can promise you that, but first I have to decide what it is I truly want. Please understand that."

Her mother nodded and tried to smile. "I'm worried about you. I don't even know where you're staying. Can you at least tell me that?"

"No, I can't. You would tell Dad, and I'm not ready to face him. You know as well as I do that he will badger me, and I will cave. Please give me the time to find the backbone to stand up to him."

Katy waited and hoped her mother would reach out to hug her. When she did, Katy raced into her arms.

"I love you and Aidan so much," her mother whispered. "You are both stronger than I ever dared to be. Go. Do what you need to do. Please stay safe, and let me hear from you soon."

"I love you, too, Mom. I'm not far away. I'll call when I can."

Katy hurried out the back door. She took a quick look at the beautiful flowers blooming in various beds throughout the backyard. Brick-lined paths edged with lush, green grass led to a section of the grounds her mother lovingly called her meditation garden. Katy followed the path to her mother's special spot and the wooden bench made from cypress skis, which Aidan had made in woodshop years ago.

Although Katy had seen it many times during the years she'd helped her mother plant and maintain the yard, today as a woman who was growing comfortable with her own thoughts and actions, she'd absorbed the meaning of the words inscribed on a brass plate attached to the back of the bench.

I come to the garden alone.

For the first time in her life, Katlyn Mays understood how true that statement was to her mother. She'd always taken care of her two children, making sure they had everything they could possibly want, putting up with the mental and verbal abuse Bill Mays spoon-fed her on a daily basis. Granted, it was on a silver spoon. But Katy now saw it as clear as the water that flowed from the miniature waterfall into her mother's goldfish pond.

Despite the time she devoted to her children, her church, her clubs, Katy's mother was always alone.

Running her fingers over the plaque, realization settled hard in the pit of Katy's stomach. Had she chosen to move forward with her marriage to Jeremy, her life would have been the same as her mother's. She fingered the ring in her pocket. No matter what decisions she made from there on, she was confident she'd made at least one right choice.

TYLER WALKED TO the edge of the pasture where three storage buildings held anything and everything that had to do with the ranch. The original structure had served as a barn for many years back when his father was a child. The second building was built shortly before Tyler was born. The third and newest was erected after the Dixie Rooster became a dude ranch. Now, all three served as a storage and maintenance facility.

Even as Tyler opened the gate to the employees only restricted area, he knew it was a ridiculous notion to hope to find a brand-new truck parked in one of the tractor bays. He'd bet his last dollar that Sid was driving that vehicle at that very moment.

Still, Tyler held onto a tiny thread of hope that his cousin had the decency to do at least one thing right for his dad's sake.

"Wow, that's two words I've never heard in the same sentence—Sid and decency," Tyler spoke to the wind.

He opened two of the doors only to find stacks of boxes, crates, old tractors, miscellaneous farm equipment, and enough spider webs to knit one hundred sweaters. The last barn was not near as messy as the other two. Things were arranged neater. Each box had a sheet of paper listing its contents and taped to the side facing outwards. That, of course, had Aunt Hilda's organizational skills written all over them.

In the far rear corner was a battered green rocker. The webbing in the seat was frayed, but still serviceable. Next to it stood a small table with a bronze horse-based lamp. Tyler turned on the light and settled onto the chair, slowly at first to make sure it didn't collapse to the floor.

Directly in front of him was a cedar chest he recognized as one Uncle Frank made for Aunt Hilda. Inside he found numerous photo albums. The first one he opened had pictures of Tyler and Sid at around six-years-old playing in an old washtub in the backyard and one of Tyler's dad spraying them with a water hose.

A large lump rose in Tyler's throat. So much of the time he'd spent with his father had faded into shadowy images and memories of recounted stories by his mother and by Uncle Frank. But the day that picture was taken remained bright and vivid. Tyler squeezed the bridge of his nose, hoping to stop the tears threatening to form. The picture was taken a couple of days before his father was killed. Being playfully sprayed by his dad was the last memory Tyler had of him. That moment was even clearer in his mind than in the picture, even though he didn't remember ever seeing it.

While he was studying the picture, a shadow splashed across where we sat. He looked up and found Katy standing in the doorway.

"I hope I'm not interrupting. I dropped the shingles off at the bunkhouse, and then I saw the door open. I figured it was you. Thought I'd see if you need any help."

"I'm not sure. I thought I'd check these barns to see if by some miracle Sid left the truck."

"I take it he didn't?"

Tyler smiled and shook his head. "I didn't really expect he would, but my trip out here wasn't a total waste. I found several photo albums that Aunt Hilda had put together. She loved taking pictures."

Katy pointed to the one Tyler had been looking at when she came in. "This looks like someone is having fun."

"Yeah, that's my dad spraying me and Sid. We had been playing in an old washtub, and he had come to the house to change his boots. Two days later, they were loading a bull to take to market. It crushed Dad against the side of the trailer.

"It's funny, but I've never seen this picture before, yet the image I see here is the only clear picture I remember of my dad. Sure, I've seen hundreds of pictures that Aunt Hilda and my Mom had, but none of them are as vivid in my mind's eye as this picture. The next thing I can remember about Dad was my first grade teacher walking me to the principal's office. There she told me that Dad was dead. I cried, and I felt ashamed that I was a big boy, and I was crying like a baby.

"One of the ranch hands picked me up from school and took me home. When I got there, Uncle Frank waited for me on the porch. He picked me up, held me to his chest, and he sobbed against my shoulder. It was then I learned there were times when a man or a boy was allowed to cry."

Katy laid her hand on Tyler's arm and could almost feel his pain. "I'm sorry your father left you so early. If he was anything like your Uncle Frank, he must have been a wonderful man."

"So I've been told, but like I said," Tyler nodded toward the album, "this is the only real memory I have of him." He stood and tucked the picture into his breast pocket.

Something deep inside Katy sensed Tyler's need to be comforted. She moved directly in front of him and slipped her arms around his waist. With her head against his chest, she could hear the tranquil rhythm of his heartbeat and the unmistakable sound of him choking back a sob.

Embracing Tyler for any reason other than to console him had not entered Katy's mind. It was an instinct she seldom acted upon. Open affection had been a rare occurrence in the house she'd grown up in, but that didn't mean she hadn't longed to be held at certain times in her life.

The sadness in Tyler's eyes and the wobble of his voice had moved her to do something foreign to her. If she wondered if he would shirk away from her, that notion disappeared when he closed his arms around her and rested his lips against her hair. Katy's body hummed with the contentment of their shared moment.

"So," a male voice boomed behind her, "I see Mother was right."

Chapter 9

THE BLAST FROM Jeremy Everson's voice startled Katy out of Tyler's embrace. She spun on her heels to face her ex-fiancé. Tyler stepped up behind her. His closeness filled her with confidence and the need to set things right with Jeremy. How had he found them in the maintenance storage building, so far away from the ranch house?

"What are you doing here?" was the first thing she wanted to know.

"I think the question is what are *you* doing here? No, wait, I guess the answer to that is fairly obvious. You've run away from our relationship to be with this hayseed. Do you really think this jackleg will be able to give you the things I can?"

Jeremy's words cut Katy deep in her heart. She quickly closed the space between them until she came eye to eye with him. She intended to attack him for calling Tyler immature names, but her brain quickly told her that wasn't the way she needed to diffuse the situation. She had to lay out the facts. And though it saddened her to have to hurt Jeremy, she had to say her piece and have it over with.

"Look, I'm sorry things didn't work out for us." Katy did feel bad about that, but not enough to overlook their many differences. This relationship had run its course long ago, and she was pretty sure Jeremy knew that, too.

"I'll leave you two alone." Tyler passed by both of them on his way out of the storage building.

"No wait," she called, but he'd already disappeared. He was right. She'd have to fight this battle on her own. She faced Jeremy again. "You only wanted me because I was your assurance of a secure and prosperous future. You are exactly the kind of son Dad wanted Aidan to be. You don't need to ruin your life and my life because you think that is the only way you will get what you've dreamed of. If you continue to adhere to Bill Mays' narrow-minded set of rules, you'll have a permanent place at the bank for a long time." In spite of being the truth, the words were bitter on Katy's tongue.

"Well, of course I will." Jeremy puffed out his chest.

Why had Katy never noticed how much he looked like an amphibian? With his dark olive shirt and pale green tie wrapped tightly around his neck, he was the spitting image of a bullfrog. Even his baritone tendency made most things he said sound like it should be punctuated with *rib-bit*. She bit the inside of her cheek to stifle the giggle clamoring at the back of her throat.

Katy had said her piece, and there was only one more thing to do. She reached into her pocket and held out her engagement ring. Jeremy stared at it for so long she began to wonder if she'd misunderstood him. Did he really care about her? Is that why he was holding back from taking it?

"I don't want that ring back." *Rib-bit.*

Caught off guard, she asked, "Why not?"

"Your father is the one who bought it. You need to give it back to him."

Katy wasn't sure she understood what Jeremy had said. It was mixed with several rib-bits echoing through her mind and words that sounded like her father had bought her engagement ring. "That can't be true. Why would he do a thing like that?" Anger flowed through her with a mighty force.

"He wanted to make sure you had a much bigger and more expensive ring than the one I bought. I wasn't going to look a gift horse in the mouth. He had your mother pick it out."

Katy put her hands to her temple and rubbed them in small circles. She'd never known the degree of sadness the last few minutes had brought her, and she wasn't sure she could handle much more. "Is there anybody in the town besides me who doesn't know my own father bought my engagement ring?"

"Yeah, my mother, and, if it's all the same to you, I'd like to keep it that way."

That was perfectly fine with Katy. She preferred no one

knew about the humiliation rushing through her veins. Her father hadn't even let her fiancé pick out her engagement ring. Oh, no, Bill Mays would have nothing short of the Hope Diamond for his daughter to flash around at the country club.

What was the foundation her life had been built on? Sadly, she had no idea.

Jeremy drew her attention back to him. "Did you hear me?" Katy hadn't heard anything except the sound of her world crashing down around her.

"No, what did you say?"

"I've changed my mind. I think it would be better if I gave the ring back to your father myself." He reached for it, but Katy closed her hand around it and shoved it into her pocket.

"I know your dad didn't mean any harm. He wanted to make sure you had a big rock to flash around. I probably shouldn't have told you about that. He's already ticked with me. Maybe I'd better take it back to him."

"Oh, no. It will be my pleasure to take care of that. And what exactly is he mad at you about?"

"Mom saw you driving around town in that beat up truck with the ranch's name on it. She made a mad dash to the bank to see why you were doing such a thing. It was then I put two and two together and figured out that when you came out here to deliver the papers, you didn't have what it took to do the job, so you decided to cross over and take up arms with the enemy."

"How dare you diminish the importance of my new job? It took a lot more courage to walk away than you would ever understand." Katy felt as if her brain had been Tasered. "And, for your information, this is not a military exercise. You are taking away a family's life without a substantial reason." There were several really bad names dancing across Katy's tongue, but she managed to corral them before she said things she'd probably be sorry for.

Evidently, George had heard her yelling. The dog lumbered in, and for a second, growled at Jeremy. "It's okay, boy. I'm not going to hurt him. Go lay down."

Jeremy frowned, then continued. "There may be a speed

bump with the foreclosure. I let it slip to Mom that your father and I are anxious to get the land because we have a developer ready to snap it up to build homes on." Jeremy looked tired.

Katy knew how vocal his mother could be. A small amount of satisfaction crept through her, and a smile pulled at the corners of her mouth. "Why did that make Dad mad? What can she do about it?"

"Nothing really major, but as the president of the Cantor Historical Society, she can put a kink in the foreclosure procedure. First, she pitched a royal fit right there in your dad's office. She told him the historical society would be seeing the judge to ask for an injunction to stop the process as soon as possible."

Dang, Katy would have liked to have seen that, but for now she'd pull her satisfaction from just knowing Mrs. Everson was on the ranch's side.

Katy's interest was more than piqued. "Can she do that?" Her insides shook, and her pulse raced. That information was something she had to know.

"Not really. At the most, she might be able to hold up the proceedings for a week. That will only be for the judge to decide if the property is really worthy of historic recognition."

Thrilled at the prospect of finding a way to help Frank keep the ranch, Katy asked, "Is it worthy of recognition?"

"It might be if Sherman slept here on his march to the sea, but he didn't. Nothing else has ever taken place here that should be remembered in history. So like I said, Mom won't be able to get it stopped completely. She'll just give the Davises at the most an extra week."

Katy accepted that as good news, but she did wonder why Jeremy was divulging that kind of information to the enemy, as he kept referring to anyone opposed to the bank. "Why would you tell me that?"

"Maybe you aren't the only one who has a heart. I don't enjoy this part of the business. But I would appreciate it if your father never found out I told you that the grace period is probably going to be stretched out an extra week. I don't want him to know."

Katy's troubled heart lightened. She and Jeremy appeared to have at least come to terms with the end of their relationship. "You don't want Dad to know what? That you've taken up arms with the enemy?"

"Exactly." Finally a smile made its way to Jeremy's somber face. At least now he looked like a happy bullfrog.

Katy nodded. She had no reason to run to her dad with such information. "So your mom stood up to my dad?"

"You should have heard her. She told him that as president of the Cantor Historical Society, it would be over her dead body that the ranch would be turned over for a rich man's profit."

"Yikes, what did Dad say?"

"He said he would make sure she had a nice funeral, and then he gave her one of his infamous hand dismissals."

Suddenly, confusion took Katy's mind for a whirl. She should be disappointed that her engagement had taken so many twists in just three days. She didn't really love Jeremy, nor did he love her. He'd used her for his selfish aspirations. Her father had paid for the engagement ring, which her mother had picked out and Jeremy had given her as a token of his undying love. But instead of being crushed or angry at this turn of events, Katy was thrilled at the outcome.

Over Jeremy's shoulder and off in the distance, she saw Tyler talking to the foreman by one of the bunkhouses. No matter how things turned out from this point forward, she knew what love felt like. Her gaze drifted back to Jeremy. And she knew what love wasn't.

TYLER FINISHED going over the projected work timeline with the foreman. The renovation crew had about two weeks of work left, and then it would be time to bring in the crews responsible for housekeeping, the kitchen duties, and ranch hands that would take care of maintenance of the bunkhouses, the stables and riding the property looking for broken fences and injured animals.

Once the guests arrived, the hands would also give riding lessons and teach some of the aspects of ranch life and horse handling. Those interested would learn how to rope and barrel race. They would also take the guests on a hayride through the trails in the backwoods and serve lunch from the chuck wagon.

At night, they would entertain guests around the campfire with music and a few tall tales. That had always been Tyler's favorite part of the day. Some of the employees already lined up had been part of the guest ranch for a long time before Aunt Hilda passed away. Thankfully, they wouldn't need training, and they would be able to work alongside the newbies.

It took a large amount of people to run a guest ranch like the Dixie Rooster. Starting out slow may have been the best way to go, but Sid had taken and spent the money from reservations on such a grandiose scale, it would take that many people to provide the special services the heads of the corporations would be expecting.

The way Tyler figured it, he had a little over two weeks to gather the money from various places to either pay off the loan against the ranch, or to fold it up and use his hard-earned money to reimburse the reservations already collected.

Tyler's life had been dropped right in the middle of a Saturday special serial at the Bijou. He had to save the ranch from the evil villain and in the meantime rescue pretty Polly from the railroad track and make her his own.

At that moment, Katy came out of the house onto the front porch. The way she was dressed caused Tyler to take a second, longer look at her. A grin eased its way across his mouth. She'd evidently done some shopping while she was in town. She'd left wearing pale blue pants his mother would have called pedal pushers and a white blouse.

Now, resting her hip on the banister and looking out across the pasture, she was every bit a cowgirl. Tyler took in each aspect of her new look: from her straw hat topping her auburn hair braided into two pigtails, slowly moving down to her short-sleeved plaid blouse, to her snug-fitting jeans, to her cowgirl boots of tan leather with inlaid pink design. Maybe all that time he'd had to listen to Beth's detailed descriptions of clothing had given him an insight into appreciating women's fashion.

No, that wasn't it at all. He didn't have to know the fashion industry lingo to know whether something was pretty or not. And after his disaster with Beth, he'd become a little better prepared to see the real person deep inside someone.

The cowgirl waiting for him on the porch was the real deal, and Tyler liked her very much. Hopefully, the guy who had interrupted him and Katy in the storage barn had not won his way back into her heart.

Tyler hurriedly closed the space between him and the front porch.

"I'm sorry about that," Katy said even before he had climbed the steps.

"Not a problem. I tried to stay close enough to be out of earshot of your conversation, yet be handy if you needed me to escort him off the ranch."

"That wouldn't have been necessary. Jeremy can be mouthy, but that's about all the more ferocious he ever gets."

"Did you two make up?" Tyler watched Katy's pretty face and selfishly hoped the answer was no.

"Not hardly. We should have pulled the plug on that relationship a long time ago."

Why that was such sweet music to Tyler's ears, he wasn't quite sure, but he gladly accepted it as a good thing.

"Anyway, would you like to go over the last few things I found on the desk?" Katy asked.

"Now's as good a time as any." Tyler held the screen door open. As Katy entered the house, she brushed against his arm. Her nearness and the sweet scent put him in a struggle with his desire to pull her against him and enjoy the inviting fragrance of her perfume. Luckily for him, she'd moved quickly into the office.

Once there, Katy motioned for him to sit in the main, cowhide chair. She stood behind him and laid out everything Tyler needed to be aware of. "These are bills that need to be paid now. A couple of them will be late in a few days." After she told him what they were for and how much was needed to take care of the necessary payments, he told her to write the checks and get them all ready to go into the mail. He would then have Uncle Frank sign them. Since they were mostly utilities, he would have those out of the way for another month.

"Once that is done, give me the bottom line total for the bank account."

"Sure thing."

Much to Tyler's disappointment, Katy took a seat across the desk from him. He would have much preferred she stayed close to him.

"Next, I found a savings account statement for a bank in Augusta. It appears to have been about two years since there have been any transactions, but back then there was over fifty thousand dollars in there. Someone withdrew forty-five thousand at one swipe."

"Over two years ago, huh? Give me the statement, and I'll ask Uncle Frank about it. Anything else?"

"Well, I'm not sure what your thoughts are about this, but here's the title to the pickup Sidney bought and absconded with." She handed it to Tyler.

He studied it hard. "The title is in Uncle Frank's and the ranch's names."

"Yes, and I doubt Sid has anything saying he has permission to be driving the truck which belongs to his father and a corporation. You can report it stolen and let the authorities bring it back for you. Hopefully, that can be done in short order, and you'll have time to resell it before the end of the month."

"That's something to think about, but we have no idea where he could possibly be. I'm sure the authorities would take a report, but it is such a common truck, I would think the chances of finding it would be slim to none. And for all we know, Sid could be in Mexico or Canada." Disheartened, Tyler rubbed his neck and leaned back in his chair. "Talk about your needle in a haystack. It's a good thought, but I think it would be a fruitless effort."

"Maybe there are a lot of trucks like that one, but not many will have these on it."

Tyler took the papers Katy handed him. "This is a bill for designing and applying two rooster logos to a blue pickup. Hmm. You know, those bright-colored roosters on a new blue truck might be easy to spot. That could make a difference in finding it. I'll call the police right away and report it stolen."

Tyler started to leave, but stopped. "By the way, you're doing a good job. I can't believe how quick you got to the bottom of this. It still has to be taken care of, but as least it's been whittled down to a manageable pile. Not quite as overwhelming."

Tyler followed Katy into the sitting area outside the office. His gaze slid down the length of her legs wrapped snuggly in blue jeans. "Are those new boots?"

She turned to face him and smiled widely. "Yes, they are. These are my new ranch duds." She laughed softly. "When I went in to pay for the shingles, they had a whole display of western wear. Since I didn't have anything like that and since I hope to be working here on the ranch for a long time, I decided I needed cowgirl clothes. I bought several blouses, jeans, and these." She stuck out her foot and proudly showed off her new boots. "To top it all off, I had to have this handmade raffia hat." She pulled the string from around her throat and lifted the hat onto her head.

With her pigtails hanging to the top of her shoulders, it shocked Tyler at how much she was the spitting image of the woman he'd put into the artwork of the ad campaign he'd been working on most of the afternoon. The woman's inviting smile in the picture he had used in the ad had caught his attention right away. With that coming so quickly to him, the rest of the ad had fallen into place.

The fact that Katy resembled the image on the new advertisement he had emailed to Beth was totally an unconscious selection, but one that now had him taking a second look at his assistant.

"As soon as I fix dinner, I have to make several phone

calls." Quickly Tyler tried to move his attention away from Katy. "How about I take care of the cooking tonight?" Katy volunteered.

Instantly, his thoughts were all about her again. Her cute pigtails.

"You can go ahead and do what you have to do."

The sound of her voice.

"I'll let you know when it's ready."

Her perfectly shaped lips.

Suddenly he realized she was waiting for him to answer her. "Oh, if you're sure you don't mind, that would be perfect."

"I don't mind at all."

Tyler quickly dragged his gaze away from her and opened the door. "I'll just get to those phone calls then." He hurried from the room before he did something stupid like kiss Katy Mason until neither of them knew which end was up.

Tyler settled into the office chair behind the big desk. First, he called the local police to report Sidney's expensive new sled as stolen. He'd like to be there when they found it and hauled his cousin off to jail. An officer would come out to the ranch in the morning and take the report.

Next, Tyler dialed Beth's cell phone number. After being switched to her voicemail, he left a message following the beep. "Beth, please give me a call here at the ranch."

While he tried to decide on another number where he might call her, he looked over the bank statement of the savings account Katy had found. What was going on at the ranch two years ago that would warrant a withdrawal of forty-five thousand dollars? That was a real head scratcher. Now was as good a time as any to ask Uncle Frank that question.

Tyler found his uncle watching television in his bedroom. Kicked back in his recliner, he was probably napping more than anything else.

"Are you up to talking about a few things? It can wait until after dinner if you are really into that show."

They both glanced at the screen. Screaming women with big hair jabbed fingers at each other on a reality show.

"When I dozed off cops were in a high-speed chase." Uncle Frank laughed, muted the sound on the TV, then flipped the lever on his chair and sat up straight. "What's on your mind, boy?"

"Katy found this in that stack of papers on the desk. It's a savings account statement. It shows a balance of five thousand dollars, but two years ago there was over fifty thousand dollars in there. What's the story on this account? Is it still active? Where did the forty-five thousand go two years ago? And, are there any more accounts like this in other places?"

"No, there's no more. I hate to even tell you about that."

A knot twisted inside Tyler's stomach. With it came the sickening feeling that Sid had something to do with this.

"I feel like such a failure," Uncle Frank said softly. "Hilda and I did the best we could to raise that boy, but we failed miserably."

"Let's get one thing straight. You did a terrific job of raising your son. What he chose to do with his life once he made it to adulthood is his cross to bear. Second, I was afraid Sid was involved in this. What does this savings account have to do with him?"

Frank lowered his head. "Two years ago, Sidney was caught transporting drugs from Mexico. The best I can understand, it was for a big haul. He was looking at several years in jail. I couldn't let Hildie's baby boy go to prison."

Was there no end to the misery Sid had put his dad through? "So what did you do?"

"Remember the two Civil War rifles Aunt Hildie's grandfather passed down to her? Turns out they were worth quite a bit of money. I sold them to a collector in Augusta and used the money for Sid's bail and attorney's fees."

"So the attorney got him off?"

Uncle Frank slowly shook his head. "No, he served about ten months, but it was less than if he hadn't had the lawyer."

"So, what was this savings account for?"

"I didn't want Sid in my other accounts, so I set that one up and put the money I got for selling the rifles into it and then used it to pay out for his defense. I'd actually forgotten about the little bit that was left."

"Well, it's another five thousand dollars to add to the bank pay off. At least there's that."

"Ty, boy, I failed as a father."

Tyler sat on the bed where he could look into his uncle's eyes. "Who I am today I owe to three people—my mother, you, and me. I spent three months out of every year with you from the time I was six until I started college at eighteen. You helped raise me. You mentored me just the way you did your own son. When I grew up, I pulled from the beliefs and values you had instilled in me. I made the choice to be the best I could be." He paused a moment to make sure his uncle understood what he was saying.

"Sidney had the same support system, the same advantages, same chances as I did, maybe more. After all, he was with you all the time. A person can blame their parents for the direction their lives take only to a certain point. After that, they are responsible for their own actions. You are not to blame for Sid's stupidity. He caused his own problems. I, personally, could never repay you for all you did for me." Tyler cleared away the lump in his throat.

"I have to ask, Uncle Frank, knowing what you did about his character: How did Sid talk you into borrowing the money to reopen the ranch?"

"He showed up here with big plans for what it would take to get it up and running again. He convinced me it was what he'd dreamed about while he was in prison. He wanted to come home and pick up where his mom and I had left off. He had a flock of estimates and projected plans for expansion. It was all professionally done. I was impressed." The dejected tone of his uncle's voice sat hard in Tyler's heart. "Or, maybe I just wanted to be impressed, wanted to see him finally make something of himself."

Just two minutes with Sid. That's all Tyler would need.

"Anyway, he convinced me that with my help at the bank, he and I could work together to bring the ranch back to life. It'd been a long time. I was very excited about the idea. It was lonely here without Hildie, or Sid, or you." Frank's voice cracked.

"There hadn't been any guests around in years. I wanted to believe him. So I did all the leg work for the large loan it would take to do everything Sid had laid out. The bank jumped at the chance to loan us all the money we needed. The head of the bank almost begged us to take even more than we were asking."

Katy stepped into the doorway. Frank and Tyler turned in unison.

"I'm sorry to interrupt, but dinner is ready."

"We're on our way," Frank said and then started struggling to get out of his chair. Tyler took his arm and helped him stand up.

Katy started to leave, but turned back. "I wasn't really eavesdropping, but I heard what you said about the bank almost begging you to take more money."

"Yes." Tyler raised an eyebrow.

"There are some ruthless financial institutes. If there is a prime piece of land they believe they can make a profit on, they gladly loan large amounts of money. If the loan is paid back, they earn high interest. If the owner defaults, the bank sells the property for a handsome profit. It's a win-win situation for them. This very well could be the situation with this loan."

"That's a startling observation," Frank said. "How do you know about such things?"

Chapter 10

KATY HAD A BIG decision to make, and she had to make it fast. She'd made a hard declaration against a banking institute, her own father's to be exact, and Frank Davis wanted to know how she knew about such things as unscrupulous loan practices.

"It's something I've learned at my—" Katy cut herself short.

"Katy has a business degree. I'm sure she learned that in one of her classes," Tyler finished.

She smiled at the two men. At least she hadn't out and out lied. She did have a degree. She would eventually have to tell the truth, but for now, she felt better just letting that ride.

"Come on. Dinner is ready."

They followed her to the kitchen. She had prepared the table with the proper place settings, table cloth, and cloth napkins she'd found in a drawer in the pantry. Three votive candles flickered a welcoming light and surrounded three perfect pink roses in a glass from Uncle Frank's garden.

"Fancy, smancy." Frank hobbled over and sat down.

Tyler waited for Katy while she carried a big bowl of salad and an even bigger bowl of spaghetti and meat sauce to the table. She'd already poured ice cold sweet tea for each of them and had a plate of grilled garlic toast waiting.

"This is really good," Frank said then took another big bite of spaghetti and sucked in one strand like a kid. "Pretty and can cook, too." He looked at his nephew and winked.

Tyler pretended not to notice, but Katy had.

"Thank you. I have to make a confession." Not a phrase she'd made lately. "This is the only thing I can cook. I hope that isn't part of my job description, because I think everyone would get mighty tired of spaghetti every day."

Tyler's bright smile warmed her entire body, and she was sure it changed the color of her complexion to a deep red.

"It's definitely good enough to have once a week and maybe leftovers for lunch the next day."

"I can certainly do that." Actually, she would enjoy that very much.

"When you called us to dinner, I was just about to tell Uncle Frank about the police report."

Katy felt like an intruder. "Should I be part of that conversation?"

"You seem to be fitting in nice around here, and you're working awful hard to get our butts out of a bind." Frank started to use a cloth napkin, but laid it back down and swiped his long sleeve across his mouth. "From what I can see and from what Tyler has told me, you have a good grasp on finances. So, I'm sure you'll keep anything you hear between the three of us. I had just finished telling Ty about my son Sidney's stint in prison for drug running."

Good Lord, what a piece of work Frank's son was. No wonder Tyler called him Sid the Snake. Katy decided right there she may have to help Tyler strangle Sid.

Tyler looked at this uncle. "Did you know Sid bought a brand new truck before he left? He paid cash out of the loan money."

"Yeah, I saw it. Pretty thing. Blue. He said he was test driving it, but once I saw the Dixie Rooster logo on the doors, I knew that was a lie. The next day was when he disappeared. I think that boy has too much bad blood from his mother's side of the family. Many years ago, two of her cousins were hung as horse thieves."

Tyler chuckled. "We just had this talk, remember? What Sid does cannot be blamed on anyone but Sidney Davis. He is responsible for every one of his actions, good or bad. Right?"

"Right." Katy agreed, but wasn't sure about that. Honesty at her home meant saying whatever it took to keep from upsetting her father. Her mother did it, and Katy followed suit. This was the first time she'd ever thought that she could make the decision to not do that. Her gaze slipped from Tyler to Frank and then back. Maybe now wasn't a good time to start being perfectly honest, but she would have to very soon.

"Well, I wanted to warn you, Uncle Frank, that I'm filing a stolen vehicle report with the police in the morning. The truck is legally yours. If we get the truck back, we should be able to sell it and use the money for the mortgage. If they find him, he will be arrested again."

"We have to do the right thing. If that is part of it, so be it." Frank's dejected reply hurt Katy deeply. As he left the room, she could almost hear his heart breaking.

She rose to clear the table, and Tyler followed suit. As she washed dishes, he dried and put them away.

"This has been quite a day. One minute I see hope for coming up with the money to pay off the loan, the next it seems like the most impossible feat ever," Tyler said.

"You're moving in the most positive direction." Katy accidently splashed dish water onto her blouse. She took the towel from Tyler and wiped away the suds on her. "I know you could definitely do it, if you had more time. That seems to be the elephant in the room at the moment, but I may have a little glimmer of hope for that."

"Great. What is it?" Tyler flung the dish towel over his shoulder, crossed his arms, and leaned against the counter dangerously close to Katy. She piddled with the last pot to buy her a moment to gather her composure.

"Apparently, Jeremy's mother saw me in the truck with the ranch logo on it. She went to the bank to ask him why. He told her he didn't know why, but he did know I wouldn't be here long because the bank was foreclosing on the ranch." Katy slipped the towel from Tyler's shoulder and hung it on the rack a short distance from where he stood.

"When she asked what they would do with the property, he told her they hoped to sell it to a land developer who would build homes on it. She's the president of the local historical society. She told Jeremy she'd been trying to get this place on the historical society register for years. Evidently, she pitched a fit right there and told him she was going to file an injunction against destroying this property."

"Can she do that?"

"Jeremy said she could, but it wouldn't do anything other than give you an extra week."

"But a week is another seven days of robbing Peter to pay Paul, or in this case the Mays Savings and Loans." Excitement laced his voice.

"If you'd like, I can check with Jeremy in a couple of days to see what Mrs. Everson did, if anything."

The telephone on the wall next to the sink rang. Tyler picked it up.

"Dixie Rooster Ranch," he said.

"Yes, I did. Give me a minute to go to the office." He handed Katy the receiver. "Will you hang this up when I get to the other phone?"

She waited until he'd left the kitchen, and then she placed the receiver to her ear. "Thanks, Katy, I have it."

"Katy? What is she doing there this late at night? Working overtime, I suppose."

"If you must know, she lives here."

Somewhere in the middle of Beth's sputtering, Katy eased the telephone back onto its cradle. Again, she wondered exactly what the story was with Tyler and Beth. So far, Katy hadn't been able to get a clear vibe on whether they were a couple or not. For at least two reasons, she hoped not.

First, she got the distinct impression that Beth's holier-than-thou attitude wasn't something Tyler should have to deal with. He deserved much better. And, second, since she'd arrived at the ranch, something inside Katy's heart told her she would be very good for him, and he would definitely be good for her.

TYLER WAITED until he heard the kitchen phone click off before he settled himself in the office and resumed his conversation with Beth. "Okay, it's your dime."

"I knew you'd come to your senses sooner or later. I just thought it would be sooner than this." Why hadn't Tyler ever noticed Beth's arrogance? Did he actually find that appealing at one time?

"I didn't call you for that. I want you to do something for me. Did you get the email I sent you this afternoon?" He deliberately put a cold edge to his voice. He wanted no misunderstandings where Beth was concerned. She owed it to him to do this one important task. And, other than that, they had nothing to talk about.

"I haven't had time to check email. I've been in meetings all afternoon. What did you send me?"

"I put together an ad to generate more business for the ranch."

"And exactly what do you want me to do with it?" Beth snapped.

"I want you to pull in some of your favors from a few of the different media outlets you've been sending your clients to. With all the business you push their way, surely some of them owe you a space in their magazines or Internet advertising with a hefty discount or maybe even do it for free."

"Are you crazy? Why would I do that for you when you walked off and left me? You won't return my calls."

"Because you owe me something for that major ad campaign you pirated from my computer and claimed as your own. Remember?" Tyler's temper grew closer to the surface with each word Beth uttered.

"Of course I remember, but I've told you over and over again I'm sorry. I was desperate and had to turn in a successful proposal immediately, or I would have been fired. You know all that. Do you really blame me?"

"No, I blame myself for being so stupid. I'm giving you the opportunity to repay some of what you stole from me. You don't have to get the creative department involved. I've done the entire ad, and it's ready to go. Surely you can dispense with your commission. That will leave only the cost of placing the ads. And, I know you feed ads to at least three travel print magazines and a couple of Internet sites. Use your winning ways to get me the cheapest price to run those ads." His demands had been made, and he expected them to be followed in quick order.

"Okay, I'll do what I can, but I'm not promising anything. Tyler?" Beth's voice turned to syrupy sweet. "Don't you miss me at least a little bit? Are you planning on coming home anytime soon? I want you so badly."

At one time, Tyler would have caved at the implication of Beth's words, but that time had passed. "That's not even in my line of thought at the moment. I won't leave here until I can't do anymore. I won't leave Uncle Frank until this mess is cleaned up."

"What about us? How can we work on our relationship with you so far away?"

"Beth." Tyler's sharp tone startled even him. *There is no us.* "We have no relationship anymore. That was over and done when you betrayed me. I know I'll have to go back to New York eventually, because I have loose ends to take care of. But that's a long way off."

"Well, I'm having something delivered to you at the ranch. I have a feeling that when you see it, you will change your mind about us. It will be a reminder of what you had with me. Good night, Sweetheart. Think of me in your dreams."

The line went dead. Tyler hung up the phone. "Sure, I'll think of you. In *your* dreams." He hated the amount of anger he'd been carrying around for weeks. Apparently he wasn't hurting anyone but himself. It was time to let it go. He needed some fresh air to clear his thoughts and let his anger subside.

Outside, the lights had come on, illuminating all the flower beds. Behind the blackness of the distant hills, the silvery moonlight shone through the rapidly moving clouds. The majestic sight brought an eerie calm onto the front porch. He'd only been out there a few minutes when Katy joined him.

"That's an unusual sky," she said.

With those few short words, Katy's tender voice settled over him and washed away the residue of Beth's annoyance. "It's a beautiful sky. This is the only place I've ever seen it like that."

Tyler sat on a rocker, and Katy took the one next to him.

"This afternoon, I finished the ad and sent it to Beth in New York. That was her on the phone. After we finished talking about the ad, she said there was going to be a big surprise delivered here. I was just standing here, trying to figure out what it could be. I know what I hope it is."

"Oh yeah, what's that?" Katy rocked gently and stared at the sky.

"Remember I told you I had made one very bad investment. It was an engagement ring for Beth. I'm hoping against all odds that she is returning that to me."

Katy hoped that was it, too. She shook her head. She shouldn't be wishing such things. Maybe Tyler still loved Beth and was hurt by the break up. Katy was a lot of things, but she truly believed being selfish wasn't one of them.

"If that's it, I'm sure I can return it for a full refund. That would be a nice chunk of change to add to what I've started calling the Robbing and Paying account."

When Katy first came on the porch, she sensed tenseness in Tyler, but if he had been lost in bad feelings, they appeared to be gone. The garden lights allowed Katy to see Tyler's smiling face, and she relaxed a little. Her thoughts had been brightened since she found out the ridiculous truth about her engagement. She'd already decided to hock the ring and take whatever money she got from it, put that with her small savings account, and pay it against the ranch loan.

Wouldn't it be a hoot if two engagement rings helped save the ranch? She stifled a giggle. Her father would never be the same if all that came to pass, and, in a roundabout way, his money helped to bail out the ranch. Now she sported a grin big enough to cause her jaws to ache.

Katy yawned. "Guess I'll turn in. This ranch life is hard work."

"I was just thinking the same thing," Tyler agreed. "I have aches where I didn't even know it was possible to hurt." He paused for a moment. "Speaking of aches, we have a hot tub. We might as well get some use out of it. Did you happen to bring a bathing suit with you?"

"No, I don't have one, but I have some shorts that might work well."

"Great. I'll meet you back here in a few minutes."

Katy hurriedly slipped out of her new western wear. From the top closet shelf, she pulled a sewing basket which she assumed had belonged to Hilda Davis. She took the scissors and cut off a pair of Capri pants she'd brought with her. Now that she had new jeans, she could make the Capris serviceable for the pool and hot tub, at least until she could buy a new bathing suit. She also had a paisley print bra that didn't reveal any more than a bikini top would. She wrapped her terry cloth bathrobe around her and hurried outside.

As they left the front porch, Tyler took Katy's hand and led her across the graveled driveway and into the recreational room a short distance away. They crossed the room to the back exit. From the bar, he snagged a bottle of wine, uncorked it, and grabbed two glasses. He flipped on a couple of switches, and like magic, the hot tub began to bubble, and the patio lights came on.

Katy climbed onto the steps, which had evidently come with the tub because they matched in material and color. As she sank into the hot water, the hassles of the day melted into the bubbles. Tyler poured a glass of wine and handed it to her. He fixed his and then joined her in the tub. He settled next to her in a form-fitted seat.

Katy couldn't quit thinking about what Tyler had said about hoping Beth was sending him her engagement ring back. That relationship was over. He was free and more than anything, she wanted his arms around her, but she couldn't bring herself to make the first move.

She sipped her wine and enjoyed the closeness of his mostly bare body. Their arms touched, and Katy leaned closer to absorb more of the gentle vibrations going through every part of her body. As if it were the most natural thing in the world, Tyler put his arm around her shoulder, and she laid her head against him.

They sat there, not moving, just enjoying the bubbling sound coming from the tub and the hum of the pool pump.

Several frogs and crickets were singing their nightly chorus. The wine was very good, but Katy couldn't blame all of her euphoric state on the alcohol. It mostly had to do with the man beside her and all that she imagined he could be.

"So this is what you are up to?" A woman's voice shattered Katy's moment.

In one fluid motion, Tyler jerked his arm away and sprang from the hot tub and faced the woman.

"What are you doing here, Beth?"

Chapter 11

TYLER COULDN'T believe that Beth had made the irrational decision to just show up, unannounced, at the Dixie Rooster Ranch. He'd talked to her on her cell phone a short time before, and she hadn't bothered to mention she was on her way to see him. Instead, she'd barged in while he and Katy were enjoying a glass of wine in the hot tub.

"I asked what you are doing here." When Tyler had jumped out of the tub, he hadn't even bothered to grab a towel. Water dripped from him and puddled around his feet.

"I came to talk some sense into that thick head of yours. I stupidly thought that when you saw me you'd forget how angry you've been, but I didn't count on your having another woman heating up in a hot tub. How could you?"

Tyler took a quick look over his shoulder to see how Katy was reacting to Beth's unexpected appearance. Katy didn't seem to be affected in any way, but how could he be sure? He wasn't sure what his own reaction should be.

With only her head and neck sticking out, one could easily assume that under the water she was naked. Tyler's stomach pitched and rolled, tangling his nerves in the process. He took Beth's arm and pulled her inside the rec room. "I don't know why you are here, but let's be perfectly clear: You aren't staying."

She shook free from his grasp. "I just paid a small fortune for a taxi to bring me here from Augusta, but I'm not going back that way. You and I are going to talk this out. You're making such a big thing out of me putting my name on one measly ad."

One measly ad? His clenched teeth were all that kept him from using words his Aunt Hilda would have torn his behind up for saying.

"What difference does it make if it has my name or your

name on it? In the end, the commission money belongs to both of us. But with me getting the credit, it kept me from being fired." Slowly and with precision, Beth took the three steps needed to put her body against Tyler's.

As quick as a snake strike, Tyler's fingers locked around her shoulders, and he pushed her away from him. "Please don't make this any harder than it needs to be. You and I are done. Totally finished. I tried to make you understand that even before I left New York to come to the ranch." He took another couple of steps away from her.

"You can put icing on a turnip, but that won't make it a cupcake. And that, Beth, is what you have tried to do from the beginning. You've made your excuses, but they cannot erase what you did. Now let's call the cab back, and maybe you can get a flight out first thing in the morning."

It dawned on him at that moment exactly how stupid and blind he'd been where Beth was concerned. What was there about this woman that made him think he could spend the rest of his life with her? Whatever it had been, he had now overcome it.

"You may think I have no say-so about anything"—Beth's demeanor took on that of a woman possessed—"but I can promise you this, I'm not leaving here in a cab or on a hay wagon, not tonight anyway. I do have to go back tomorrow, but I want you to properly escort me to the airport, and I hope you will be leaving with me."

Tyler supposed he had no choice but to make room for Beth to spend the night. Maybe they did have some things to talk about, like when he would go back to New York, and what part of the things they'd bought together would he take with him when he cleaned his stuff out of the apartment they'd shared for two years. And maybe, just maybe, he could broach the subject of the engagement ring. Slow and calm would be his motto.

"I have to check on something. You wait here. I won't be but a minute." He stepped through the door and onto the patio.

Tyler expected to find Katy still in the hot tub, but the wet footprints on the concrete leading around the corner of the building told him she must have gone back to the house. He certainly owed her an apology for deserting her when he had dragged Beth inside. At that moment, he hadn't known what else to do. Right now, though, he needed to deal with the irate woman waiting for him. Since Katy had been surprised when her ex showed up, surely she would understand the position in which Tyler had found himself in.

FROM THE FRONT porch, Katy could easily see through the waist-high windows of the large building guests used for meetings and various games like pool and darts. Tyler and Beth were squared off, face to face like sparring partners. First he would volley words in what Katy could only guess from the expression on his face was high volume, and then Beth would loudly return with her thoughts.

She couldn't hear them from the porch, but despite being surrounded by the noise of a million bubbles gurgling around her, she had heard about every other word while in the tub, which made getting exactly what was being said indiscernible. Probably if she had strained her ears, she could have heard what Tyler said to Beth, but Katy hadn't wanted to hear any of that.

When Beth had arrived, humiliation had wrapped Katy like a scratchy wool robe. She had practically thrown herself at a man she'd only known a few days, and until the moment his girlfriend showed up, she wasn't even sure if he had one.

Beth.

A shiver climbed Katy's spine. Once Beth had showed up, Katy knew she should have given Tyler the same respect he'd shown her when Jeremy came by. She should have gotten out of the tub and gone into the house to give them some privacy. But there was no way she was going to expose herself to any more disgrace by making a hasty retreat in her homemade, cut-off Daisy Dukes and a paisley-print bra. No, it was better to stay put beneath the water line and be thought naked than to give Hotsy Totsy Beth more ammunition to toss into Tyler's face.

So Katy had waited until the coast was clear. Now she

needed to get to her bedroom and stay out of the way, if at all possible. And while she did that she needed to find a way to ease the growing ache in her heart.

"Did that fancy lady find Ty?" Frank called as Katy passed by his bedroom. She stopped just outside his door. He looked comfy in his recliner. "I wasn't sure if you were out there somewhere with him. I was going to ring the bell so he'd come to the house, but she wouldn't let me do that. She saw lights on the building across the driveway. She said she'd go check for herself to see if he was over there."

"Yeah, she found us." Katy thought it best to leave out the where and how Beth had discovered Tyler. "Can I get you anything before I head to bed?" she asked.

"Thanks, but I'm fine. Do you think Ty will be okay with that woman?"

Katy was fairly sure Tyler could hold his own. "Why do you ask?"

"Even though she was dressed like she stepped out of one of those fancy magazines my wife used to read, that woman also looked like she could bite the butt off an angry bear."

Katy waited to hear that gruff chuckle of Frank's that she found very pleasant and contagious, but it didn't come. Actually, she didn't feel much like laughing either. "Okay, I'll retire for the night."

Once in her room, she started to lock the door, but decided she was being a little paranoid. She hadn't locked the door one night. Why would she do that now? Because Beth was a little different from the Georgia women Katy knew? That was a ridiculous reason, but just in case, she pushed the button on the door knob and locked herself away from the boogie man or woman, in this case.

Katy heard Tyler and his guest come into the house. They were talking low, so their words were muted. At least their tones sounded more amicable and not so much like they may go to blows.

Katy took her shower and dressed for bed. She decided a glass of milk would taste good. She quietly opened the second door in her bathroom, the one that Hilda Davis used to slip into her kitchen early in the morning. After she poured her milk, Katy grabbed the box of Oreos from the pantry.

Once back in her sanctuary, she sat at the desk in the corner and ate her bedtime snack. She'd just about finished when she heard footsteps in the hallway and the unmistakable sound of the door opening in the next room. Tyler's room. It wasn't long before she heard him and Beth talking. Katy could only take that to mean they were going to bed.

Together?

Her heart needed consoling, so she did what made the most sense to her. She quickly ate three more cookies and washed them down with the last of her milk. As fast as possible, she went to the bathroom and brushed her teeth. Once the lights were out, she got into bed.

With her pillow wrapped snuggly over her ears, Katy refused to listen to the goings on in the next room. They were none of her business. It was her own fault if she felt the least bit jealous. She should have better control over her heartstrings.

KATY WASN'T SURE how long she'd been asleep. She would guess not long by the fuzzy feeling in her head and the weight of her eyelids. She looked up and realized someone was standing by her bed. Chills piggybacked their way through her whole body. A scream would help, but she couldn't force it through her constricted throat.

The light from the kitchen spilled into her bathroom and ultimately into her bedroom. Her brain knew she should move, but her arms and legs weren't cooperating. Somehow she found the strength to sit up.

There really was someone by her bed.

Beth.

Katy scrambled to turn on the light and was happy to see the woman's hands were both empty. No weapons.

"Is there something I can do for you?" Katy put her feet into her slippers and pulled on her robe. "Is there something you'd like from the kitchen?"

"No, there isn't, but there is something I need to tell you . . . Katy, is it?"

She nodded.

"Well, Katy, I'm sure you think you've found your cowboy, but you need to know Tyler is mine." Beth crossed her arms over a sheer negligée that left little to the imagination. "I'll admit we're going through a rough patch, but it will be over soon. Tonight I reminded him what he's been missing, and although he isn't going with me in the morning, he'll be back to New York before long, leaving you behind."

Beth's implied statement about her reminding Tyler what he'd been missing sent a double-edged sword completely through Katy. Angry that the woman dared to attack her and frightened by the stab of jealousy which niggled in the pit of her stomach, her emotions fought a raging battle inside her. Should she engage in a childish display of words like—he's mine, no he's mine? Quickly, she decided against it, mainly because she didn't know if he was Beth's or not, but Katy knew for sure he didn't belong to her.

"And just in case you happen to see my engagement ring, which by the way, cost more than you could possibly hope to make in a year, I gave it back to Tyler for one reason." Beth shook her finger in Katy's face.

She was doing all she could to keep from biting that stubby digit with the fancy French manicure right off Beth's hand. Something in her tone served as a sharp reminder of the way Katy's father delivered his demands. She'd made a major step to free herself of being talked down to, and she certainly had no intentions of letting a total stranger with a screwed up perspective of reality talk to her like that.

Katy opened the door to the hallway. "I think it's best if you leave my room." Her strong, demanding tone surprised her, but in a strange way also empowered her. She stood her ground and stared directly into Beth's eyes.

"How dare you tell me what to do in my fiancé's family home?" Even angrier now, she carried on with her tirade.

"When he comes back to New York, and make no mistake about it, he will come, he is going to propose all over again."

Katy's staunch resistance to let Beth get under her skin faltered. But only for a moment. Either way, Katy wanted her out of her room and hopefully, without incident.

"As soon as I get back to the city, I'm going to start making plans for our wedding. It will be beautiful. You should come. I'm sure you're a big enough person to put the past behind you and wish Tyler and me the best." Beth's sneer melted into a strange, thin-lipped grin.

Katy's response was to smile slightly. "That might be a nice trip, thank you." She gave a Vanna wave, pointing to the opened door.

Without another word, Beth went back to her room. Katy quickly went to the bathroom to secure the door that goes into the kitchen.

"How in the world did she know she could get to my room through there?" Katy wondered aloud and tightly wrapped her robe around her to ward off the chill now making her tremble.

Besides being a little creepy, Beth's unwarranted diatribe raised Katy's blood pressure. Maybe the delusional woman thought she had the right to dictate Tyler's moves, but she certainly had nothing to do with what Katy felt or who she wanted in her life. She would be the one to decide what was best for her. And Tyler Davis might just be the very best.

THE NEXT MORNING, Tyler crawled off the lumpy sofa. He tried to stretch the knots and aches from his muscles, but apparently they would be with him at least for the morning. Last night when he'd showed Beth to his room where she would sleep, he gathered the things he would need to shower and clothes for the early morning trip to Augusta he would be taking when he transported Beth's carcass to the airport.

She'd given the engagement ring back to him, and he hadn't had to ask. She did say she wanted him to bring it with him when he came to New York in a few days. He could then propose, and they would start from where they had left off.

It might snow this summer in Georgia, too.

He'd done all he could to convince Beth there was no hope for them as a couple. How she processed that was up to her. She had balked a little at having to ride that long distance in Old Blue, with faded paint and decals, dents and rust spots racing to see which would bring the truck down first. In the end, she'd climbed into the cab of the truck. Tyler would have sworn she had an imaginary cushion under her butt, because she looked like she wasn't even sitting on the well-worn seat.

He managed to get her on an early morning flight and agreed to wait with her. Although he engaged in small talk when necessary, his mind was on Katy and how she had felt about all the commotion at the ranch the night before.

KATY HAD WATCHED from her bedroom window as Tyler helped Beth into Old Blue and put her luggage in the back of the truck. If she knew she was only staying at the ranch for one or two days, why had she brought so many suitcases? Katy had spent a month at Camp Cryer in Cleveland, Georgia, when she was twelve and hadn't taken but two small bags, neatly monogrammed, of course.

The old truck's engine had to be turned over a couple of times before it started. Katy had said a silent prayer it wouldn't stall and make it necessary for Beth to stay another day. Katy still hadn't been able to process her late night visit or to decide if she should tell Tyler about it. For now, since the main problem was on her way back to New York, Katy would focus on her job and vigilantly look for signs that Tyler's heart wasn't on its way north, too. After all, maybe Beth had been able to show him what he'd been missing.

Her position at the ranch had already given her more pleasure than she could have ever had at the bank. Each morning, she awoke with the excitement of a child going to summer camp. She loved her job, and by the clock on the wall it was time she got to it.

She stopped by the kitchen for a cup of coffee. Frank wasn't there, but there were three bowls in the sink. Before leaving the kitchen, she washed up the few dishes and put them to drain on the sideboard.

She popped into the office to turn the computer on. On the sofa, a sheet and a blanket lay in a crumpled mess. For Katy, it was a comforting sight. It definitely gave her hope that last night Beth had been riding high on wishful thinking. As Katy folded the bedding, a warm sensation floated from her heart to her lips. She glanced at her reflection in the window. Yes, that smile really brightened her face.

Out on the porch, Frank was sitting in a rocking chair. "Good morning, little Missy. I hope you had a peaceful sleep."

Katy wondered about telling Frank that Beth had visited her in the night, but she decided against it. The woman was gone, and that was all that mattered. "It was fine. I stayed in bed a little later than usual this morning. Now, I've got to get to work. I'll be in the office if you need me."

Grateful for the stack of things that would keep her from thinking about what was happening between Tyler and Beth, Katy dove into her work. She paid all the bills that Tyler had approved. Envelopes, statements, and checks were paper-clipped, ready for Frank's signature.

She worked on gathering all the information she could on all assets. Apparently Hilda had been very thorough when she was taking care of the bookkeeping for the ranch. Until six years ago, everything was in neat, organized files. It was only the purchases and disbursements since that time that lacked attention.

Compiling an inventory list was not a major undertaking. Katy figured she should be able to do a partial from Hilda's records and then while physically locating the equipment somewhere on the ranch, she might be able to add things that weren't already listed. That would be a big job, but Tyler and Frank needed to know what the ranch's net worth was, whether it was lost to the bank or stayed in their possession.

Katy took a few minutes to glance through the ranch's

history book. The pictures and information were very thorough and interesting. She took advantage of learning more and more about it every time she had a few minutes to spare.

After she printed out the preliminary inventory list, she placed it on a clipboard and gathered it and the mail and went back out front. It had been almost three hours since she'd talked to Frank. She could see him near bunkhouse number one talking with the workmen. Suddenly there was an eruption of laughter from the small group of men. When it all died down, Frank saw her standing on the porch. He started her way, so she went to meet him.

"I just need you to sign these checks, and they'll be ready to be sent out." Frank took the clipboard. When he'd finished signing the checks, he handed it all back to Katy. "What do you do when you have mail ready to go?" she asked.

"We have a mailbox out at the road. We put it in there before three o'clock, and Rasty Boyer will pick it up, if he ain't dead."

"Not dead?" Katy wasn't sure how to take that.

"Rasty's been on this route for fifty-five years and never missed a day. Everyone around here always says that's how they'll know when he's dead—when we don't get our mail."

There was that infectious laugh Katy loved. She giggled, too, happy for the reinforcement that she had something to smile about. "Good one, Uncle Frank. You're a card. Think I'll walk these out to the road. Be back shortly."

"I'd give you a ride, but the only thing here is the lawn mower."

"It'll do me good to walk some." Katy started down the driveway to the long entrance road that came from the main highway. The crepe myrtles lining the roadway cast shade where she walked. As she neared the first bend, a flock of blackbirds flew away from the pasture on her right. They startled her for a second, but she recovered quickly.

How beautiful everything was. Freshly painted white fences surrounded the green pastures. When she looked back at the brown log house with green shutters and other buildings all painted barn-red, they were all backdropped by a bright blue sky and Coffey's woods. Katy smiled. She'd just learned about the forest on the ranch. A couple of hundred years ago, a trapper named Jacob Coffey had claimed the area as his own. To this day, the trees around the original house were still referred to by his name.

Katy continued her trip to the mailbox. The bridge which crossed over the stream had a plaque posted that said, *Constructed in 1924. Conifer Creek.* She hoped she might find who built the bridge and how it got its name. She was pretty sure she could. The history book, though not in chronological order, appeared to be very thorough. Surely she would find it in there.

Once she placed the mail in the box and raised the flag, Katy looked back at the road. It was at least a half mile long. And the air was hot, and she was sweating. It certainly looked a long way off. She'd only gone about halfway back when she heard an automobile behind her. Moving to the side, she turned to see who it was.

"Hey, hitchhiker, want a ride?" Tyler pulled Old Blue to a stop. His wide smile spoke volumes to Katy. He was happy, and that brought her pleasure.

After rounding the front of the truck, she climbed into the seat. Before she could even think about what was going on, Tyler put his hands on each side of her head and pulled her to him until his lips crushed against hers with a passion that sent her head spinning.

Frantic, she pulled away from him. "Stop," was the only word she managed to say before he hungrily recaptured her mouth.

Chapter 12

RELUCTANTLY, TYLER pulled his lips away from Katy's. The Georgia heat was even hotter inside the old truck, but when he'd seen her walking along the road that led to the main house, all he could think of was how much he wanted to kiss Katy.

Somewhere in their kiss he thought he'd heard the word *stop*.

"I'm so sorry," he said, his breath coming in short bursts. "Did you say stop?"

Tyler looked deep into Katy's eyes. He expected to see fear or anger since she'd wanted him to quit doing something that felt wonderful to him. Instead, there was a cute sparkle in her eyes and a smile pulling at the corners of her mouth. He willed his heartbeat, hammering in his ears, to be quiet so he could hear Katy's sweet voice.

"I'm just gun shy, I guess." She ran her fingertip across his lips. His skin tingled at her touch. "Every time we make physical contact, one of our exes magically appears. It happens so quickly, I keep checking to see if they used smoke and mirrors."

"I know what you mean, but as for me, I don't have any more exes. How about you?"

Katy placed her finger to her temple as if having to think about the question. "Hmm. No, I think we're good to go."

Katy's full lips finally broke into a beautiful smile, and she moved closer to him. Placing her hand on the back of his neck, she raised her open lips to his. The warmth and sweetness whispered through him to touch his soul.

With his arms around her and with one swift motion, he turned her and pulled her into his lap. She emitted a low sound, which caused Tyler to think he'd hurt her. He pulled back and opened his eyes. Katy's eyes were open, too, and her gaze scanned his face as if it were the first time she'd really seen him.

Her eyes drifted closed again. Tyler placed light kisses on each of her eyelids, her nose, and was just a second away from tasting her sweet, pink lips when he glanced through the windshield and saw Uncle Frank standing in front of the house frantically waving his crutch through the air.

"What the heck?" Tyler nudged Katy from his lap. He nodded toward the road ahead. "Uncle Frank needs me." Tyler slammed the truck into gear and took off to the house. Old Blue may be old, but he could fishtail over the gravel and kick up a mighty cloud of dust. In a matter of seconds, they skidded to a stop.

"Jeeze, boy, the house ain't on fire. You could have driven at a half normal pace." Frank dusted his jeans with his hat.

"What's wrong?" Tyler rubbed his thumb over his lips. They were warm, and when he licked his tongue over them he could still taste Katy.

"Got a phone call, missy." Frank leaned in the window and talked to her. "I thought it might be important." He sounded a little irritated. He looked back at Tyler. "There is no need to kill Old Blue."

"I'm sorry." Tyler leaned over Katy and opened her door. "Go catch your call." Once she was out, he parked then walked back to his uncle.

"I couldn't figure out why you weren't driving up here. Everything okay with you two?"

"I like Katy a lot." Frank's gaze moved back up to meet Tyler's eyes. "And, I would never get in between you and whatever filly is tugging at your heart, but you've just come off a rocky road, and from what I understand, so has Katy." Frank shooed a fly away from his face. "Both of you need to take a good look at what is motivating this rapidly moving buggy and be sure it's not going to lose a wheel in the middle of a pile of horse dung."

"I'm—"

"Giving and receiving advice doesn't warrant a debate. You know what your intentions are. I've given you my old man's advice. Do with it as you will."

Tyler watched his uncle wobble up the walkway to the house. Once the confusion cleared, he was able to let the older man's words sink in. Tyler couldn't argue with the logic. Things had moved faster than they should have, but he wasn't sure that was all his doing. Katy appeared to be okay with . . . with what? A couple of innocent hugs and a short session of demanding kissing with a side of unbridled passion?

What exactly was that longing he felt each time he looked at Katy? Surely he couldn't be trying to replace Beth with the first woman who came along. That couldn't possibly be it, because he had never experienced this excitement with Beth. He'd thought they had been on the same track with their lives. They'd shared very little of the same interests outside of work. She loved opera at the Met. He loved the Mets. He'd go with her to the evening galas. She always begged off from going to the ballgame with him, because the sun was hot and made her sweat, and the extended exposure would ruin her skin. Duh.

Foolishly he thought their careers were the dominating factor in the relationship that would hold them together. It turned out his career was his, and hers was hers. Every man for himself. Guilt kicked him in the pit of his stomach. He was as much responsible for the end of their relationship as Beth. If asked if he loved her, Tyler would have to say he wasn't in love. He was in comfort. He was comfortable and too lazy to work at making it great or ending it all together.

Now that he'd found himself in the middle of a completely different lifestyle from what he had in New York, he couldn't believe how the knots in his neck and shoulders had eased into aching muscles from the various jobs he'd taken on while getting the ranch in order. He rather enjoyed those aches. They came with a feeling of accomplishing something through hard work.

The threat of losing the ranch if he didn't cover the mortgage had given him a burning passion to see that didn't happen. He glanced at the house. Katy was standing at the office window which faced the driveway. With the phone to her ear, she appeared to be in deep conversation. Tyler hoped it wasn't bad news. Something that wouldn't take her away from the ranch and . . . from him.

He decided not to disturb her. Yesterday, he'd intended to mow the yard surrounding the house, but he kept getting sidetracked. By the sun's position, he knew he had about two hours before high noon. That was as good an excuse as any to steer clear of Katy until he could think through Uncle Frank's wise words. He pretty much knew what was in his heart, and no amount of sage advice was going to change that.

AS KATY LISTENED to Jeremy's voice through the telephone, she watched Tyler out the front window of the office. After a short conversation with his uncle, he'd stood in one spot, looking around as if wondering what to do next. For a short moment, their gazes had met. She offered a smile, which he returned.

"Thanks for calling, Jeremy." Katy tried to cut it short, but he evidently had a little more to say.

"Can I ask you a question, Katy?"

She couldn't begin to guess what that might be. "Sure. What is it?"

At that moment, she watched Tyler turn and head in the direction of the maintenance area. She looked him over from the top of his black hat, down past his nice-fitting jeans to his brown leather boots with inlaid snakeskin. There were no signs he'd been living in New York City for several years. He looked every bit the part of a rancher in the heart of the south.

"I was wondering." Jeremy brought her back to reality. "Are you happy living out there on that ranch?"

Katy didn't have to think about it. Her answer came quickly and straight from her heart. "I'm very happy. I've never experienced anything like I do here. From the time I get out of bed in the morning until I'm back in it at night, I am surrounded by hardworking, fair-minded people, and seeing what Mother Nature can do is . . . I would say a dream come true. But the truth is I never knew there were places like this to even dream about."

From somewhere in the distance, Katy heard a lawn mower coming closer and closer. Finally, it came into the front yard. Tyler's tanned, bare chest rippled with well-defined muscles. Evidently, sitting behind a desk wasn't all he did. Katy imagined him going to a gym either before or after work. However his body had come to its present state, she liked it and had a hard time listening to Jeremy and not pressing her nose against the window pane.

"So," Jeremy said, "you're living a life you never thought about before, yet you are happier than you've ever been. I don't know if you'll believe this or not, but I want you to be happy, and if it is way out there in the country, and you get to be a true Dixie Cowgirl, then I wish you happiness."

His words touched in a very special way. "Thanks, Jeremy. I want you to find happiness, too." She swallowed the lump in her throat. "Give my best to your mom. Tell her I appreciate what she tried to do. Goodbye, Jeremy." She didn't wait for him to say goodbye, mostly out of fear he would have more questions. She wanted to give some thought to what he'd called her—Dixie Cowgirl. That name fit her very well, and she liked it.

Katy turned back to the window. Tyler's bare chest glistened with sweat. A warm tingling sensation wrapped her completely. Was this what it was like to truly long for someone? To want more than anything to be captured in the arms of someone who already held your heart and soul?

She took one more glance through the window. He may be riding a lawn mower instead of a powerful steed, but to her he was her Dixie Cowboy.

She thought she'd take advantage of a few minutes of free time by going through the history notebook. Every time she looked at it, she discovered a new and exciting fact about the ranch.

Out in the reception area, she heard Frank's crutches hitting the floor with each step he took until he was in the office and sitting across the desk from Katy.

"I'm real proud of the way you've helped Tyler get a grasp on what exactly has been going on around here. I know I should have been smart enough to do it myself, but some of this fancy stuff like that computer goes right over my head. Sidney was doing all the banking on that fool thing, and I never saw any paperwork. That certainly is no excuse for the mess I let this place get in."

"There isn't much that can be done about the past, but more and more every day, Tyler's goal to gather enough money to set it all right becomes more obtainable. He has made a plan and so far, it's going good. Thank you for your kind remarks, though, but truthfully, I'm having the time of my life."

"I'll bet you are," Frank said and then smiled widely.

She wasn't sure what that meant. He definitely didn't say it with malice, it was just a statement, but it sounded like there was a hidden meaning in there somewhere. One she thought better left alone.

Frank threw his crutches out of the way. "I have two pieces of advice for ya."

"Oh, yeah, and what would those be?" Katy smiled.

"Don't get old, and don't get hurt. And, for Pete's sake, don't get hurt after you get old."

"I'll try to remember that." Katy giggled. "Is there something you need me to do? I would rather you tell me what needs to be done than for me to putter around looking for things."

"I got to thinking about something this morning, and I thought I'd talk to you about it." Frank leaned forward and rested his arms on the desk.

Since this looked like it might take a while, Katy sat down, too.

"Those wooden file boxes over there." He pointed to a bank of desk-high cabinets under the front window.

"Yes, sir, do you need something out of one of them?"

"Inside those are all the files my sweet, organized-to-the-hilt Hildie had compiled before her death. There are files after files of anything and everything anyone would ever need to know about the operations of the ranch when it was a guest ranch."

Excitement moved Katy to the point she thought she might have to stand up and yell, but she restrained herself. "That's wonderful. If it's okay with you, I'll start going through them right away."

"Sure, that's why I mentioned it. I tried to talk Tyler into not putting so much time and energy into getting the guest ranch back up and running. But he is determined to do all he can to save it and to make sure it is ready for guests due here in a couple of weeks."

"I know. He's not spending any more money other than wages, utilities, and food. Most of the renovation is done, and he said by the time the working staff is due to come in he'll know if he's going to be able to gather all the money. At that point, he'll make the decision to bring them back and move forward, or to fold it up."

"If there's a way, Ty boy will do it. He has all the stubbornness and determination of his father and the heart and soul of his mother. He's a good one, he is."

How wonderful that Frank could see Tyler for what he truly was worth. That certainly wasn't anything she or Aidan had ever gotten from their father. Even though Katy had long ago covered the hole that had left in her heart, every once in a while, she was painfully reminded it was there. "I see parts of you in him, too. And I know he thinks the world of you," she said to Frank.

"He was easy. His cousin, on the other hand, was ornerier than a wild boar being chased by coon dogs."

Suddenly, Tyler stood in the doorway. "I'm going to take a quick shower to get the grass and dirt off of me. After that, I thought we could fix a picnic lunch and ride out to the north pasture. Would you like to go with me?" Tyler looked directly at Katy, but Uncle Frank answered.

"I don't think my leg is good enough for me to get on a horse, but thanks for asking." He turned to Katy. "Why don't you go?"

Tyler shook his head and rolled his eyes. "Good idea, Uncle Frank. Wish I'd thought of it."

The old man picked up his crutches, and as he left the office, he said, "I don't want anything to eat. I'm taking a nap."

Tyler and Katy shared an intense smile. "He's a mess, isn't he?"

"I think he's adorable."

"When I saw you standing at the window while you were on the phone, you certainly looked upset. I hope everything is okay."

She thought for a moment. "Actually, no it isn't."

A worried look crossed Tyler's sun-kissed face. "What's wrong?"

"I told you that every time you touch me one of our exes interrupts. That call was from Jeremy."

"That's a little scary." Tyler leaned across the desk and stopped only a few inches from her lips. "I'm willing to take a chance." Softly, he placed his lips on hers. She lightly pressed her hand to his cheek and welcomed his kiss, savoring the sweet tingles in the pit of her stomach.

When they pulled back to look into each other's eyes, the phone rang. Simultaneously, they released a defeated sigh.

"So help me, if that's Beth, you might want to cover your ears. I'm not sure I can control my tongue." Tyler reached for the phone.

Katy hurried past him. "I'll go fix lunch."

"Thanks," he called over his shoulder, and then put the phone to his ear. "Dixie Rooster. May I help you?"

"Hi, Tyler. This is Carrie. Please hold the line for Mr. Fleming." Carrie Rickey was Connor Fleming's personal assistant.

The residue from their last conversation still left a bitter taste in Tyler's mouth. He'd tried to tell Connor that Beth had out and out stolen the big ad campaign and presented it as her own. Their boss had insulted Tyler by telling him he was disappointed by his display of sour grapes.

"Sour grapes, my—"

"Tyler, how are things going in the hot south? I bet you're about ready to get up here and get things back to normal."

"And by normal do you mean working my tail off for a company that has no appreciation for my time, energy, creative talent? I'm sure you can guess my answer. What can I do for you, Connor?"

"I need you back at work as soon as possible. We just picked up a client who needs your expertise. It's a big deal, Tyler. It'll mean quite a bit of money in your pocket. What do you say? Can you be back here by day after tomorrow?"

For a split second he contemplated doing it, but quickly overcame his lack of better judgment. A big bonus would help on his ranch bailout, but it would take too much time to prepare a presentation. Time he needed to keep the work at the Dixie Rooster progressing forward.

"I honestly don't know what's going to happen here, but right now this is where I'll be. Thanks for the offer, but it's a *no*."

The one thing Tyler did know was he needed to make a quick trip back to New York. He had to get his stuff from the apartment. Funny, but when it came down to it, that's all you could call it—stuff. He couldn't even remember what was there that he couldn't just walk away from, but he needed to at least get it out of Beth's way. There should have been a couple of automatic deposits made from residual accounts from the firm. Just a little bit here and a little bit there that required attention. Yes, he could do it over the phone from right there on the ranch, but not as quickly nor as final as if he flew up there and took care of it all first hand, in person.

But the most important thing on his mind was to try to return the engagement ring Beth had given back to him. He'd originally bought it from a client who dealt with the finest diamonds. It was more than he could hope for that the jeweler would take it back and refund all his money. Tyler didn't even expect that. There would be a restocking fee, depreciation, and probably a fee to remove any fingerprints left on the flashy ring. Whatever he could get would go to better use for the ranch than being used to draw attention to Beth's two hundred dollar manicures.

TYLER HAD SHOWERED and caught up with Katy in the kitchen. She put two cans of soda into a bag.

"What can I do to help?" he asked.

"I think I have it all put together. Deli turkey sandwiches, celery and carrot sticks, and a sleeve of chocolate crème cookies." Katy threw a handful of napkins in with the rest of the picnic things. "I take it that wasn't your ex who interrupted us."

Tyler smiled widely. "No, that was my boss wanting to know when I was coming back to work." He scoffed, but Katy thought that was a really good question.

"What did you tell him?"

"I told him I wouldn't be back to work until things were settled here."

So, that meant he would be going back to New York eventually. Katy's heart sank. It was silly of her to think he would give up the excitement of the big city and his high-powered career to come back to the country life of manual labor, blood, and sweat. Absolute foolishness, yet she didn't fully believe it was all her imagination that the hot Georgia days and warm breezy nights fit him as comfortably as her new cowgirl boots fit her.

She looked up into Tyler's face and realized he'd been watching her standing in the middle of the kitchen floor lost in her own thoughts.

"I'm sorry, did you say something?"

"No, the expression on your face looked like your brain was doing battle with something. Anything you'd like to share with me?"

Chapter 13

STANDING IN THE kitchen, Tyler had asked Katy if she'd like to share her thoughts with him. She already felt silly enough when he'd caught her zoned out thinking about him going back to New York permanently and how much she hoped that didn't happen. But to tell him how she felt about that wasn't something she could do for a while.

"I was just thinking about how exciting it is to go horseback riding again."

Not a complete lie.

From the kitchen counter, she picked up the picnic lunch she'd made for her and Tyler to take on their ride out to the north pasture.

"Well, let's get going." Tyler stepped aside to let her go first. "By the way, you never said what Jeremy wanted."

"I'll tell you when we get outside," she whispered.

"Might as well tell him now," Frank yelled as they passed his door.

Katy and Tyler both made abrupt stops. "You don't even know what we are talking about." Tyler stepped into the room.

"Since Katy was speaking all hush-hush, must be something she doesn't think I should hear, but we both know you'll tell me later anyway. So, as that commercial on TV says, Whazzzup?"

Katy laughed out loud. "You are so funny. Did Tyler tell you about the historical society trying to get an injunction?"

"Yeah, he did." The old man smiled.

"Well, the president of the society went to the judge this morning about that. In the papers she presented to the judge stating why this ranch shouldn't be destroyed, there were the papers from years ago when you and Mrs. Davis refused to let it be marked as an historical site." Katy stepped into Frank's room.

"The judge said if it wasn't important enough to you back then, it wasn't important enough for him to try to save it now."

She stated almost all of the facts of what had happened that morning as relayed to her by Jeremy, but left out the part about the judge being her father's first cousin. However, she did experience a sharp pang of uneasiness about what would happen when Tyler found out who she really was.

She stole a quick glance at Tyler, and for the first time the full effect of that reality hit her squarely in the heart. Her feelings for Tyler were growing stronger by the day. Yet, the truth she'd hidden from him since the day she arrived at the ranch could be a deal breaker for anything resembling a future for them.

"You're looking a little sad, missy. You don't need to feel bad, because Hildie would be spinning like a top if this place was declared an historical site, because they would restrict things we could or couldn't do to comply with their rules. She never wanted to be a member of their club." Frank leaned back in his recliner. "I appreciate the thought. Now, where ya going on your picnic?"

Tyler eased closer to Katy. "Mrs. Perkins called earlier and said she noticed a hole in the hog wire fence back of the north pasture. We're going to go out there and check it out."

"There's a fairly new four-wheel ATV in the storage shed attached to the back of barn two in the maintenance area. You should take it. It hasn't been started in a while."

"An ATV?" Tyler rubbed his temple.

"Yep. Sidney had to have it. It's a glorified golf cart, if you ask me."

Tyler looked at Katy with a desperate, questioning gaze. She shrugged. "I'm afraid it's true. That's one of the things on the inventory list we need to locate and assess. I don't remember the number off the top of my head, but they weren't giving them away the day Sidney bought it."

Tyler placed his hand in the small of her back and led her down the hallway. As they reached the porch, he sucked in an audible breath that sounded like it was his first in a long time.

"Tomorrow we will start the inventory process, which I

now understand has an ATV. Today, however, we'll take Shiloh and Lady for a ride."

ONCE THEY ARRIVED in the north pasture, Katy and Tyler stopped in front of the old house, and he dismounted first. With her hands on his shoulders, he took Katy by her waist and lifted her, slowly allowing her body to slide down his chest. Her nearness sparked a fire deep inside him, urging him to pull her closer, daring him to act upon the undeniable desire growing between them.

Too soon, Katy broke their connection and backed slowly away from him. An unexpected cool breeze swirled around Tyler, making him aware of how intense the heat from their bodies had truly been.

"Time to eat." Katy sat on the concrete carriage steps in front of the old house. Together, she and Tyler ate in silence and had almost finished their last bites when she thought of something she'd wanted to know.

"Why is the Dixie Rooster called a guest ranch instead of a dude ranch? They do the same thing and serve the same purpose, right?"

"In a way, but Aunt Hilda said a dude ranch conjured up images of dudes poking cows. Her guests were ladies and gentlemen. She wanted to treat them with the utmost respect and Southern hospitality." He swiped his mouth with a paper napkin. "Even the tables in the chow hall were covered with cloth tablecloths and linen napkins. Real china and silverware. No paper products for her guests."

"Sounds wonderful. I wish I could have known your aunt."

"She would have liked you." Tyler tucked a strand of Katy's shiny auburn hair behind her ear. She stared into his eyes. Her tender gaze fueled the desire already burning inside him. His brain fumbled to remember what they'd been talking about. Finally, it came to him.

"And you would have liked Aunt Hilda. She made everything fun. They used to have square dances in the rec room every Saturday night. The guests and a few people from the surrounding area would attend." Tyler took a big swig of his cold drink.

"The man who called the dances used to sing a song about *Cute Little Katydid*. It went something like 'It wasn't what Katydid that made his knees grow weak. It was what Katydidn't that swept him off his feet.'"

She smiled sweetly. "Funny. My brother Aidan always called me Katydid." She knew her voice grew strained when she talked about him, and that was the main reason she did it so seldom.

"Where is your brother?"

"I don't really know. He and my father had a terrible fight. Before he left, he said he was going to find a way to work with special needs children. I haven't seen or heard from him since." She tightened her jaws in an attempt to ward off the tears. "I guess he figured I would be better off if I didn't know where he was." Now that she'd moved on with her life, her brother was the only thing missing to make it complete.

"He and Jeremy were good friends. I'm sure they've stayed in touch. I always figured that if he had problems, I would know from Jeremy." Katy forced a smile, but inside, the reminder of how her dad had dictated the way things would be in her life cut her deeply. The saddest part was that she had allowed it to happen.

"How long has that been?"

"Almost three years." Her voice trembled slightly.

"That's a long time."

"Sometimes it seems forever." Katy gathered the remains of their lunch and put it back into the bag. Wanting to move off the subject of Aidan, she asked, "Now what are we going to do?"

"You see that path there?" Tyler pointed to a swath of trampled shrubbery that ran along the side of the old house. "The horses or some large animal has been tromping through here, and I have a feeling that at the end of this little trail is the broken fence Mrs. Perkins called about.

You can wait here if you like."

"No, I'll go with you."

Tyler unhooked a leather drawstring bag, which he'd placed on his saddle horn before they had left the stable. He shoved it into his back pocket. Katy followed behind Tyler and tried not to scream when a fly-away spider web latched onto her hair. Tall trees with their branches intertwined formed a canopy with no sunlight allowed in. The heavily shaded area gave her an eerie feeling. When she tripped over a kudzu vine and released a stifled grunt, Tyler reached back and captured her hand. He pulled her safely through a narrow opening into the bright sunlight. Katy squinted until her eyes adjusted.

"Yeah, here's the break." Tyler dropped her hand and shook a rotted fence post which crumbled at his feet. The wire fence had been rusted for several years and just fell away from its support, leaving an opening not big enough for a horse to get through, but there were hoofprints in the red clay which told Tyler one had at least tried to escape.

He pulled the remains of a fallen tree to the busted fence. Katy grabbed a branch and helped him. Together they jammed it as hard as they could into the opening to close the hole.

"Thanks," he said.

"No problem."

That would have to do until he could get the crew out there to do the repairs. The fences along the front of the ranch were all wooden and whitewashed bright white. Those appeared to have been taken care of before Sid took off, but he would have to check the line around the back of the property. It looked like they would need new posts and hog wire. And, several long days of hard work, not to mention an outlay of cash they didn't need to be spending right now.

Back out in the open pasture, Katy shaded her eyes and looked out over the beautiful meadow. Particles of dust mixed with sunbeams danced over the green grass. Sporadic patches of yellow flowers and horses grazing freely completed the perfect picture of heaven on Earth. With the sound of the creek rushing over the river rock and an occasional butterfly landing nearby, it all took Katy's breath away.

"This certainly is awesome. I expect that since you were raised here, you don't see the beauty."

Tyler gazed out at the scenery. "You would be wrong. I've wondered every day since I've returned this time how I ever left this place. I would . . ."

He pointed at a group of horses. "See that horse over there by the creek? He's limping." He took Katy's hand. "Come on."

He gave her a leg up, and then he mounted, too. As they got closer, it was easy to see that they in fact had a lame horse on their hands.

Quickly, Tyler got down and hurried to the poor animal. The horse backed away. "Whoa, boy. I'm not going to hurt you. Let's see what you got going on here."

Masterfully, he ran his hand down the horse's right front leg all the way to its fetlock. He found nothing wrong there, but when he raised its foot, he found the problem immediately. A spike of rusty wire lodged in the horse's hoof.

"That's gotta hurt, huh boy?" Tyler pulled the tool bag from his back pocket and handed it to Katy. "Would you give me the pliers in there, please?"

"Sure." After she handed the tool to him, she held the horse's foot so Tyler could pull the wire out. It didn't appear to be an easy job.

"Wow, that's in there pretty deep. It's going to hurt. Grab a hank of his mane to keep him steady, but be ready to get out of the way if he balks. I don't want you hurt, too."

"I'm okay. Go." She was happy to be helpful.

Tyler pulled with all his might, and the spike came out. The horse flipped his head up and bolted backwards. Katy let go of everything she had been holding. Tyler lunged and captured his own handful of the horse's mane. With his other hand, he stroked the animal's neck, all the while talking in a low, smooth tone with encouraging commands. "Settle down. It's okay now. Hold still."

Katy watched in awe as the horse reacted to Tyler's gentle directives. It was as if the horse understood he was in able hands and reacted accordingly. What an incredible gift Tyler had. How amazing it would be to spend the rest of her life with a man who was so gentle and caring and could calm an injured animal with his soothing voice.

He looked Katy's way. Her heart pounded hard against her chest. Tyler was exactly the man she wanted to be with forever.

Frantically, he searched the ground and kicked the bushes.

"What are you looking for?" She moved next to him.

"I need something to put around his neck so we can lead him back to the stable. There's no way to get him to follow us. We'll have to call the vet. That wound will have to be treated. He'll also need a tetanus shot."

"I know something that will work. You wait right there." Katy went behind a big oak tree. When she came back, she put out her hand which held a navy blue bra with a touch of white lace along the top edge.

Tyler stared first at her chest, then quickly shifted to the intimate apparel. The sight of the bra brought a suggestive smile to his lips which hit Katy in her stomach and rocketed heat to her cheeks. When his gaze snapped to her, she realized he really didn't know what her intention was. A brand-new sensation filled her. She couldn't remember ever flabbergasting a man before. But she certainly had given this cowboy cause for reflection.

While trying to hide her smile, Katy put the bra around the horse's neck and then slipped the back strap through an armhole. She handed Tyler the strap. He adjusted the makeshift lead and then pulled it snuggly near the horse's ear.

"That works for me," he said.

Once Katy was back on Shiloh, he handed her the reins of his horse. She was glad they were slowly making their way back to the stable. That allowed her to ride comfortably without her bra. A full gallop might make for an awkward ride.

Once he had the horse secured in a stall, he handed Katy her bra. "That was pretty clever. I don't think I would have ever thought of that."

Only slightly embarrassed, she took it and gathered it into a ball. "I can't take all the credit. I have a friend, Maria, who has horses. We accidently let one out of a corral. We chased it forever. He was having a ball, running and kicking up his heels. Maria and I just knew for sure the horse was laughing at us.

"He finally stopped to eat, and we caught up with him. We needed something to lead him back, so Maria used her bra. I thought it was crazy at the time. Glad I stored it in my bank of things I may need to know someday."

TYLER CALLED THE veterinarian who had serviced the ranch for over twenty years. Dr. Grant had arrived quickly to tend to the lame horse. The doctor worked closely with Tyler to make sure all the instructions were written in plain language so he could either take care of it or pass the responsibility onto Norm Walls, who had been in charge of the stable and horses for many years during the time the ranch was in full swing.

When Uncle Frank shut down the ranch, Norm had retired. But when Tyler had called him earlier that afternoon and explained that he had to go back to New York to take care of some business, Norm agreed to come out of retirement and maybe longer, if needed.

The doctor had treated the horse's wound and had found a spot in the tack room to finish writing down his instructions.

Tyler tried to occupy his mind with grooming the horse they'd just brought from the pasture, but when he began to brush the animal's neck, he could think of nothing but Katy taking her bra off. Once he realized what she wanted him to do, he appreciated the inventive idea, but before that his mind was doing backward flips like a circus performer.

Since Beth had always prattled on for hours about fashions, their functions, their materials, and then insisted that Tyler answer questions like it was a pop quiz, he had learned a lot about women's clothing. Out there in the pasture, when he had first looked at Katy's bra, his instinct had been to shout, "Navy blue bra, white lace, B cup."

Thankfully, he hadn't done that, which would have confirmed he was a complete idiot. Of course that was better than the second thought that raced through his mind—*does this mean she wants me to run my hand under her blouse?* Now that would have been embarrassing.

WHILE TYLER TOOK care of the injured horse, Katy explored the files Frank had told her about earlier that morning. He certainly hadn't exaggerated a bit. Hilda Davis was one organized woman, and for this, Katy was thankful. She didn't know anything about hospitality management or food services, but with Hilda's help, Katy was sure she could learn from a master.

Hilda's files contained menus, recipes, beverages, and the amounts needed per person. There were detailed reports about decorations for the tables, what recipes were liked best and liked the least. She had inventory lists of linens, flatware, and china and stemware.

Where in the world were all these things stored? Now would be a good time to ask that question. She hadn't seen Frank since she returned from the north pasture with her bra in her hands, but she knew that Tyler was in the stable with the vet.

She made a copy of the catering inventory, then secured it on a clipboard. She had one more thing to do before she went in search of Tyler. She found what she was looking for without much effort. If she hadn't yet impressed Tyler with her investigative ability, she thought this would do the trick.

Armed with her clipboard, she went to find Tyler. She found him in the stable currying the horse. She reached over the gate and scratched the animal's nose.

"Do you know this horse's name?" she asked.

"I don't. Remember, I haven't been home for six years. They got rid of a lot of the horses, but I have no idea which ones they kept."

Katy tapped her finger on the top file. "I have copies of bills of sale for about fifty head. What I think happened is that Hilda had a complete list, but after she passed away, Frank sold off all but the fifteen or so they still had left. Each horse has a picture and lineage, whether they were thoroughbred or not. I think this is the one you brought in today." She handed Tyler the picture.

He looked at it and then the horse, checking the white markings on his chest and left rear foot. "I think you're right." He handed the picture back.

"His name is Chalmers. He's been on the ranch about seven years," Katy told him.

"That's great. You're pretty handy to have around." His big smile warmed her completely and gave her hope that she would be around for a long time to come.

"By the way"—Katy showed Tyler the inventory list of catering supplies—"where did your aunt store linens and china for when she served large groups? Do you think Frank or Sidney got rid of all this?"

Tyler looked it over for a few seconds. "I doubt it. Everyone came back to the ranch after the funeral. Mrs. Perkins and several of the other ladies from the community fed all of us. It went without saying that paper plates and plastic forks would not be used at Hilda Davis' wake. They would respect her in the same fashion she had treated all her guests. I'm sure that was the last time any of that was used."

The sweet thought of Hilda's friends and family respecting her that way brought a tear to Katy's eye. Wouldn't it be a wonderful thing to feel that much love from so many people?

Quickly she moved back to the subject at hand. "Where do you think it would be stored?"

"During my days here, I always worked outside. I didn't have much to do with the kitchen. Things like that are probably in the storage room behind the bar in the cook shack." Tyler shrugged. "When we had guests that was where all the cooking and eating was done."

"Tyler." Dr. Grant came out of a tack room at the end of the stable and started walking toward them.

Katy spun on her heel and started outside. "I'll go check out the cook shack." She made a rapid retreat before Tyler could stop her. He'd wanted to introduce her to the veterinarian.

Oh well, I can do that later.

"Here you go." Dr. Grant handed Tyler a couple of sheets of handwritten notes for taking care of Chalmers' injury. "I'll be back in two days. In the meantime, these are the things that have to be done in a timely manner. If you have any questions, give me a call."

"Thanks. I'm leaving in the morning to go back to New York for a couple of days, but Norm will be here."

"Uh oh, yanked him out of retirement, did ya?"

"I barely got the question out of my mouth before he said *yes.*"

The doctor chuckled. "That little lady that just left here, she looks familiar. Who is she?"

Chapter 14

"SHE'S MY ASSISTANT. I hired her a couple weeks ago," Tyler said, answering Dr. Grant's question. He thought Katy had looked familiar. Tyler folded up the sheets Dr. Grant had given him and stuck them in his pocket.

"I don't know much about her family, but she is from one of the neighboring towns, and her last name is Mason." Just saying those words made him realize he didn't know much about Katy at all—her family, where she came from, how old she was. If he was pretty sure he was falling in love with her, maybe he needed to ask her some of those questions.

Dr. Grant touched Tyler's arm. "Are you okay?"

Tyler swallowed hard. "Uh . . . yeah. Sure."

Or I will be as soon as my brain processes the idea that I might be in love. Was that as crazy as it sounded?

"Just have a lot on my mind. Sorry about that. What were you saying?"

"Nothing really. I just said that Miss Mason looks like someone I know. I just can't place her." He offered his hand to Tyler. "No big deal. It'll no doubt come to me later. Have a safe trip to New York. I'll keep in touch with Norm while you are gone."

HILDA HAD TO be the most organized person who ever walked on Earth. In the storage room behind the bar and right next to the big industrial-size kitchen in the cook shack, Katy had found a treasure trove of all things necessary to entertain a multitude of people. She could possibly put on a dinner for the President of the United States on a grand scale.

It was getting late, so she would tackle the job of counting everything as soon as she and Tyler finished with the ranch equipment inventory. On one shelf were piles of neatly folded white sheets. She picked up one bundle, shook it out, and discovered it held a flat and fitted sheet and a pillow case. There were no labels on them to tell the size, but they looked like they might fit one of the twin beds in the bunk house. She wanted to spread one set onto a bunk to determine its size and, at the same time, inspect for moth holes and stains. She was sure they would all have to be washed before guests arrived, but for now just making sure they were serviceable for the bunks would be her first step.

"Find everything?" Tyler blocked the door of the storage room.

"Yes, I did, and then some. This is like a butler's pantry in the old plantation homes. It's nicely stocked." Katy moved closer to the door, and Tyler stepped aside to let her pass. Her shoulder lightly brushed his chest. She could feel him watching her, and her heart turned over in response. She moved quickly into the open dining room.

"If it's okay with you . . ." Katy looked into Tyler's beautiful blue eyes, and for a moment her knees nearly gave way. Her voice took a moment to return. "I'd like to figure out what we should have on hand to feed everyone we already have reservations for. As it gets closer, then we'll see what is missing and take care of getting it here. No sense putting out the money until we are sure the loan can be satisfied."

"That makes sense." Tyler strolled over to the old juke box. "This certainly brings back a ton of memories." He moved it away from the wall and plugged it into a receptacle. "This is where we had the dances on Saturday night that I was telling you about. Sometimes we had a live band. Usually Gabe Lawson and his Band of Blowhards. They played all kinds of brass horns. But the dances I liked the best were the ones where we put quarters in the juke box and did line dancing. Especially when I got to be sixteen or seventeen and all the pretty, teenage girls came by to do the 'Boot Scootin' Boogie.'" Tyler did a few steps, shuffling his cowboy boots across the concrete floor.

After running his hand over the glass covering the old forty-five RPM records, he dropped a quarter in the slot, pressed a couple of buttons, and the room filled with a song Katy was sure she'd heard before, but wasn't sure what it was or who was singing it. Country music wasn't played at her house. When she was in college, she seldom listened to anything other than classical.

"Have you ever done the Texas two-step?" Tyler took her hand and led her to the middle of the floor.

"No, but I've seen it on television."

He swept her into a closed position like she had learned about in the ballroom dancing lessons she had taken at the Cantor Country Club. However, back then, her body had never tingled when it came in contact with those boys like it did when Tyler touched her. This was completely different, special, and she welcomed it from her heart to her soul, but shyness made Katy step back. "I have never been very good at dancing."

"Just hang on and follow my lead. It's just a short series of steps—quick, quick, slow, slow. If we are moving, and I want you to stop, I'll press both our hands on your hip like this."

Holding Katy's hand and resting it on her hip, he pressed gently. "That's when I want you to put on the brakes and stop. Concentrate on the movement of my hands against your body."

That won't be a problem. Unfortunately, thinking about and feeling the press of his hands anywhere on her wreaked havoc with the ever-growing fire in the pit of her stomach. And just exactly what was she going to do about the ache even lower in her gut?

Tyler pressed more buttons on the juke box and then took Katy in his arms. Except for the hammering of her heart, which seemed to fill every part of her body, they stood quietly in a beginning dance pose and waited for the music to begin. When it did, Tyler moved Katy around the floor, counting the two steps, leading her with gentle hand movements. At times, she was sure her feet had left the floor, and she floated over it. He made it fun, easy, and sensual.

Katy would always remember the entire day she'd spent

with Tyler, on a ranch in Georgia and learning a new dance with an exceptionally gentle and caring man. She feared her heart might burst. Nothing else could make this day more perfect.

The music stopped, but Tyler continued to hold her. Looking up into his smiling face, she plainly saw desire in his compelling blue eyes. She pushed aside a swath of black hair that lazily hung on his forehead. Even in the diminishing light, the beautiful raven color of his hair shone like silk. The tender nerves throughout her body urged her to run her fingers through it, but her brain rebelled. Reluctantly, she stepped away from his hard, inviting body and turned on the overhead lights.

"It's getting late. We better check on Uncle Frank. It's way past dinner time for him." She glanced at Tyler. "What about you?"

"I'm fine. I'll probably just have a peanut butter and jelly sandwich later. And, I looked in on Uncle Frank before I came out here. He ate a sandwich and was happy, and I quote, 'as an ant at a fourth of July picnic.'" Tyler's laugh pulled Katy along with him. Doubled over with laughter, tears rolled down their cheeks.

Contentment and joy filled Katy's heart. "I really love this place. It brings me more pleasure than I could have ever imagined." Suddenly, she remembered one of the things she wanted to do that night. She picked up the sheets she'd found in the butler's pantry.

"I want to take a minute to see which beds in the bunkhouses these sheets fit." She held them up and then laid them on a table near the door.

"We can do that in a minute. I just wanted to tell you that I'm glad you like it here. And, you're definitely good for the ranch. You're smart." Tyler took a step toward her. "You're knowledgeable about business." And another step. "And you're beautiful." He put his arms around her and urged her to slide hers around his neck, which she did, but not until she'd run her hands over his hard chest and slowly felt the warm skin from his throat to the back of his neck.

With her senses pulsing, she watched his clear blue eyes

turn darker. Instinct alone told her the midnight blue coloring was the window to his passion. As their lips met, her breath caught, and heat pooled low in her belly. His gentle kiss, warm and moist, made her long for more. Rising on tiptoes, she pulled his lips harder against hers and enjoyed the fire coursing through her veins. She could hear the rhythm of her heartbeat speaking to her—*I love him, I love him, I love him.*

Tyler lessened the hungry hold he'd had on Katy. She brushed her lips across his cheek and then trailed gentle kisses from his ear to the base of his throat. He wasn't sure if the moan he released was audible to her, but he was sure she felt the tremor of his body against her.

More than anything he had ever learned, ever suspected, or ever wanted to know, Tyler was positive he was in love with the beautiful, caring, slip of a woman who was making his body take on a life of its own. And in that life, he wanted to lay Katy down and make love to her like no other woman he'd ever been with.

By the way she made his heartbeat strum through every nerve in his body, he knew without a doubt she would be a dream worth waiting for.

He broke free from their embrace, but held tight to Katy's hand. He grabbed the sheets off the table and pulled her out the door. "I think now would be the perfect time to find out which bed these sheets fit." Tyler looked at her and smiled a knowing grin. "We may have to try several beds to be sure."

KATY AWOKE WITH the sun shining way too brightly around the edges of the curtains in her bedroom. Bolting upright, she looked at the clock. It confirmed what she already suspected. She'd overslept. Not that she punched a time clock, but she had been in the office and starting her workday by eight each day. At eight fifteen, she wasn't going to make it on that particular morning.

An unexpected smile pulled at the corner of her mouth, and her body warmed at the thought of Tyler's gentle touch and demanding lips. Maybe she had a little job security since last night she'd slept with the boss. As wonderful as it had been being held by the most perfect man in Georgia, panic flickered through her. What if their shared moments of passion hadn't meant the same thing to Tyler as it had to her? She swallowed a knot in her throat.

As quickly as possible, Katy dressed in what she had come to think of as her uniform of the day—her new jeans, a cotton blouse, and her cowgirl boots. The night before, she had washed her hair and gone to bed with it wet. That left her no choice but to brush it into submission and tie it back into a ponytail.

Out in the hot summer air, Katy found Uncle Frank sitting in a rocker watching a dust cloud rising from the road leading to the main highway. From where she was standing, she had a hard time telling what kind of vehicle it was until it left the gravel drive.

"Tyler's taken off already this morning?"

Uncle Frank handed her a folded piece of paper. "Yep. He said to give this to you."

She unfolded it and found a short and disturbing note from Tyler.

Katy, Sorry I didn't get to say goodbye. I had to go back to New York. Tyler.

"He's gone to New York?" Disappointment painfully squeezed her heart. Was Tyler going back to Beth?

"That's what he said. Something sure built a fire in his hind quarters. He was packed and scatting out of here before I could say . . . well, *scat.*"

This time, Katy couldn't find relief in the old man's humor. It was hard to speak with sadness constricting her throat.

"He had left once and then came back to get that ring he'd given that other woman. He did say to tell you he might be bringing back a surprise."

"He never gave you any idea what that might be?" She knew how downcast her voice sounded, but she couldn't clear away the lump choking her.

"I have my suspicions, but can't say for sure." The old man's voice sounded tired.

Katy took a hard look at Frank. "Are you feeling okay?" she asked.

"I'll be doing better when I can get my legs back. I'm getting soft sitting around watching everyone else work. I'm itching to get at it, too."

"I'll bet you are. I'm going to the office. Holler if you need anything." Katy took one last look across the pasture to the highway that would take Tyler to the airport in Augusta. Soon he would be in New York with the woman he'd given an engagement ring to and at one time had asked to spend the rest of her life with him.

The night before when he had made love to her, Katy would have sworn she was the only woman on Tyler's mind, but with his sudden departure, she wondered if he'd come to the realization that it was Beth he loved. She had point blank told Katy he would come back to New York with the engagement ring, and he would propose all over again to make things new. He had turned around to come back for the ring.

Was Beth right? Had Tyler decided she was the woman for him? Although he had not told Katy he loved her, she couldn't believe she'd misread all the sensational vibes that had streamed through her, filling her completely with her cowboy's love.

No, she refused to put any credence into negative thoughts. She had work to do, and she would go as fast and as hard as she could all day. When bedtime came, she'd be too tired to think of anything but sleep and lying in Tyler's arms.

BEFORE HE LEFT Augusta, Tyler had called his best friend, Ed Barber, who waited at the gate when Tyler disembarked the plane in New York.

"Thanks for picking me up." He put out his hand to his ol' buddy, who took it, pulled him into a man-hug, and gave him a hard slap on the back.

"Glad to do it. I'm glad you're back. Things haven't been the same at Casey O's Bar without you." Ed took the only carryon bag Tyler had. "Let's go get your luggage."

"This is all there is." Suddenly he realized he hadn't told his friend he would only be in town that day. "I'm only here to take care of some business, tie up a few loose ends, then I'm headed south again."

"Sorry to hear that." The expression on Ed's face showed he spoke the truth.

Tyler had been so tied up in his own thoughts of getting things closed out in New York as quickly as possible so he could get back to the Dixie Rooster and to Katy that he neglected to make his intentions plain to his friend.

From the airport to the apartment Tyler had shared with Beth, he and Ed spoke very little. They'd been friends long enough that he knew Tyler would tell him what was on his mind when he was good and ready. At that moment, Tyler was glad they had that understanding, because he wasn't ready to tell anyone that he'd fallen head first into a sweet pile of cotton candy named Katy. Just thinking her name warmed him completely.

He had tried to force himself to keep his mind on everything he had to do in a twenty-four hour period instead of flooding his mind with the magnitude of happiness and satisfaction she had given him when they made love the night before.

In his eyes, no woman had ever been so perfect. The way her bold stare had slowly raked over his naked body caused rolls of thunder to crash through all his pulse points, exciting him in ways he'd never dreamed possible. He analyzed every reaction he had to Katy's looks and touches. He had to be sure the attraction growing so quickly between them wasn't just sexual.

When her lips closed over his, and he claimed her body completely, he knew without a doubt, that even though it had been such a short amount of time since they'd met, he wanted her for a lifetime.

AT THE APARTMENT, Tyler filled a couple of suitcases and a few boxes with his personal belongings. Funny, he'd never given any thought to how much of the six rooms he'd shared with Beth were all about her. At least it made packing quick and easy.

Although he had let her know he was coming back to cut the last few strings tying him to New York, he hadn't told her exactly when that would be. He hoped to be out of there before Beth came home from work.

Tyler had stacked the last of his things near the door, and Ed had made a run down to his car, which was parked in Beth's rented parking space. When the door opened, Tyler figured it was Ed, back for another load, but he was wrong.

"Tyler, what a surprise." He spun to find Beth and his ex-boss Connor Fleming standing in the door. "Why didn't you let me know when you were coming?"

"It was a quick decision. I didn't really have time to let anyone know." He walked toward her and Connor. It had taken a while for the pieces to all fall together, but in that few seconds, reality settled in, and Tyler gave himself a mental head slap.

"Wow. It's two fifteen in the afternoon, and you two have left work early for a . . . what? Board meeting? Maybe you're planning how to steal someone else's work. This answers so many questions, like why you took her side against me when you knew I was telling you the truth. Yes, it's clear as can be now." Tyler searched his mind for the proper name to label the two cheaters, stealers.

Suddenly his mind snapped shut to any of that. He knew Beth for the conniving woman she had always been, yet he had stayed with her, professed to love her, and even asked her to marry him. He had no one to blame but himself. Although the facts had leveled a major blow to his ego, he could go back to Katy without the slightest sliver of guilt over leaving Beth.

"Did you see Ed downstairs? He was parked in your parking space," Tyler asked.

"No, my car is in the shop. We came here in a cab." Beth had the nerve to bat her fake eyelashes at Tyler and gave him her all-too-familiar look of a dying sheep in a hail storm.

Thankfully, that no longer worked. As he lifted the last box and opened the door, Beth stopped. "Even if our engagement is broken, I'd like to have my ring back."

Tyler stared at her for a long moment. "Yeah, I'd like to have my dignity back, too, but neither of those things are going to happen."

BY EIGHT O'CLOCK that night, Tyler had checked into a hotel, and he'd crossed almost everything off his extensive to-do list. The jeweler who had sold him the engagement ring had agreed to take it back less a ten percent restocking fee. He had been able to get funds from a couple of his investments. He chose the ones that didn't carry a stiff penalty for early withdrawal.

He had officially resigned from the agency where he'd worked and gathered checks due him from residual accounts. He'd had all the monies put into a cashier's check made out to Mays Savings and Loans.

He'd gone to Ed's house where he repacked everything. Whatever he couldn't get into two suitcases, he boxed up and left there for his mother and stepdad to drive into the city to pick up for him.

As he was proudly marking things off his list, his cell phone rang. Glancing at the caller ID, he was happy it was someone he'd called earlier and was beginning to think wasn't going to call back.

He pressed the button. "Hello, Jeremy. Thanks for returning my call. I have a big favor to ask you."

Chapter 15

FOR KATY, SLEEP hadn't come as easily as she had hoped. She'd worked hard all day to keep her mind on anything but Tyler. Yet, every move she made, everything she touched brought sweet memories of being in his arms and thinking of nothing but his caring, gentle hands on her body.

Yesterday morning, shortly after she'd read Tyler's note telling her he had to go back to New York, Katy had gone to the storage room in the cook shack and started counting linens for the beds. Opening the first set, her mind vividly pictured Tyler spreading a sheet on a bed in bunkhouse number two and then easing her onto the mattress.

"No, Katy, you can't think of any of that." Maybe verbalizing her admonition would make it more real. But it was true. She had to concentrate on inventorying everything she could without Tyler's help. They would count the equipment, horses, and larger assets after he returned from New York.

"If he comes back."

Katy's mind and heart were in a bitter battle. One she couldn't settle or shake. Did she imagine the strong connection she and Tyler had formed even before they'd made love? She refused to believe she could have been led astray that easily. No, she not only felt his love surrounding her, but she saw it in his eyes.

Reading and rereading the short, hand-scribbled note Tyler had left for her gave her no real sense of what was going on or what was expected of her. *Sorry I didn't get to say goodbye.* Was that a forever goodbye? Katy couldn't see him just going away and leaving his uncle all alone. Yet, *goodbye* carried a finality she wasn't ready to accept.

I had to go back to New York. Did that mean he wasn't coming back? If so, he hadn't said what he expected her to do. Did this all mean the ranch was going to fold, and she should start looking for another job? Surely he would have said that in plain English.

At the end of the first day without Tyler, he hadn't called. Her heart ached, yet she wasn't sure she had the right to feel that way. Tyler had never said he loved her. He had never made her any promises. He'd only known her less than two weeks. What kind of strong bond or devotion did she think could possibly have developed in that short time?

Now, twenty-four hours later, Katy sat at the kitchen table, drinking coffee and making her list for the day, but her thoughts continued to search her soul for answers to what she truly felt was going on in Tyler's world. When she couldn't figure it all out, she blessed all the negative feelings and set them free. That would have to do for now, because guessing was not working out for her.

"Hard work has always brought me a quiet, peaceful mind." She glanced at her list. "If I get all this done, I should be in a coma by sundown." She chuckled out loud.

"Glad to see you are in a happier mood than yesterday." Frank's unexpected appearance startled Katy.

She clutched her fist to her heart. "I didn't hear you come in. Sorry, guess I'm a little preoccupied with my to-do list." She held up the piece of paper she'd been writing on.

"You can't kid a kidder. You were thinking about Ty, weren't you?"

Katy didn't try to hide her embarrassment by denying it, but she wasn't about to tell him all of it. "Yes, I'm just a little baffled by the quick turn of events. Tyler's note was so short, it left me with so many questions I can't seem to answer on my own, like will he be back, and if so, when? If he comes back, how long will he stay before he goes back to New York?"

Did his disappearing act mean he'd chosen Beth over her?

"I know he'll be back, but when and for how long, I don't know the answers to that. We'll just have to wait and see. Unless I miss my mark, I think you and I both have two wishes."

Frank's smile brightened his weather-beaten face.

"What do we wish for?"

"That he does come back to stay and that he doesn't bring Miss High-and-Mighty with him."

TYLER HAD INTENDED to get out of the city before noon, but by the time his rental car was delivered to him, and he'd loaded all his worldly possessions from Ed's apartment into the trunk and back seat of the red Nissan Altima, it was well into the afternoon. It would have been a hard push to make it back to Georgia in one day even if he had gotten on the road early in the morning.

By nine thirty in the evening, he gave up and checked into a motel. After he'd showered, he lay across the bed, telling himself he would only rest for a couple of minutes before he called Katy. But when he opened his eyes and looked at the clock, it was almost midnight. Too late to call the ranch.

He'd missed Katy so much since he'd left home. *Home?* That was the most pleasant thing he'd thought of all day. He would be going back to the only place he'd ever dreamed of living. And Katy would be there, too. He'd longed to hear her voice and to tell her about the things he had accomplished since he'd left there. But when he'd called earlier, no one had answered the phone, not even Uncle Frank. He'd left a message, but then remembered he hadn't told Katy the password to retrieve messages. He'd tried to teach Uncle Frank how to use the machine, but he didn't have any interest in learning something like that.

Well, Tyler would try again tomorrow. Surely he would catch them then. As soon as it was confirmed the ranch was ready for guests, he'd have to reactivate the phones in the out buildings. Once the ranch had closed, they had no use for all those telephones.

He assumed Katy was doing inventory of the sheets in the bunkhouses where he'd tried to help her the night before. The thought of how he'd helped brought a smile to his heart and a yearning low in his stomach.

He fought the sheet to get comfortable and tried his best to go to sleep, but nothing worked. Finally, he gave up, and at four thirty in the morning, he started the last leg of his trip back to Katy. Expectation and longing made the trip seem never-ending. By the time he crossed the South Carolina-Georgia border, breaking the speed limit was the only way Tyler drove.

Just as anxious as he was to make it back to the ranch, he was also eager to put New York and his deceptive life with Beth behind him. Even thinking of her caused sourness in the pit of his stomach. Not because he didn't believe her capable of having an affair, especially one that involved advancing her career. No, that wasn't what made him think he might throw up. That came from the major slap to his ego that he'd been stupid enough not to realize she'd been making a fool of him.

He'd always prided himself on being a good judge of character and being able to see the real worth of a person. Katy immediately came to his mind. Of course, he was able to spot honesty in a person. Just because he'd lost that with Beth, didn't mean he'd lost it forever. It had only been for a short amount of time. He shook free of the embarrassment caused by her unfaithfulness and longed to hold Katy, the woman he truly believed he could trust for the rest of his life.

ON THE THIRD morning of Tyler being gone, Katy did a thorough job of cleaning the main house. She dusted, vacuumed, and scoured toilets, but nothing kept her from thinking about Tyler.

At breakfast, even Frank seemed a little concerned that his nephew hadn't called to check on him and Katy. "Surely we will hear from him today. Even when he lived in New York City he called at least once a week." Frank took a sip from the mug with a picture of the Big Apple skyline on it. "If we don't hear from him in a little while, I'll see if I can find his cell number around here. I don't believe I ever had to call him on his cell."

If Frank was concerned, then Katy felt vindicated for her

thoughts of all the bad stuff that could have happened to keep Tyler's doings and whereabouts so private. After all, he was a fellow human being, her boss, and for one night he'd been her lover. And now, she had no idea where he was or what he was doing or who he was with.

Since things were looking less and less hopeful, maybe she should move her concentration from Tyler to what would be her next move if her job was pulled out from under her by her father's bank. She'd seen the ranch's bank account totals. Yes, there was enough in there to pay salaries and other expenses to get it opened in just two short weeks, but there was nothing there to pay the mortgage.

Tyler had made her privy to his plans for gathering the funds needed. He'd called in several favors, had closed out as many investments as he could without being charged astronomical penalty fees for early withdrawal, but at last count that was a long way from completely raising the funds to satisfy the loan.

She took the broom out the front door. After sweeping away all the dirt and the occasional leaf from the porch, she watered the flowerbeds in the yard. She'd just turned off the hose when she saw a cloud of dust swirling around a vehicle making its way from the highway up the drive.

"Lordy, we need rain." Katy shaded her eyes against the glaring sun.

The red car stopped in front of the house. Katy walked down the path to greet the guest. Tyler got out of the car, and in a very few steps he lifted her and swung her into the circle of his arms.

"I've missed you," he whispered in her ear.

This didn't feel like the arms of a man who had just left another lover in another state. When he pulled back, and she got a good look at his face, every ounce of doubt she'd been experiencing disappeared in an invisible cloud of smoke. It was gone, and her heart hammered against her chest like a bird wanting to escape into the beautiful world that was now Katy's.

Tyler released her and pulled her by her hand into the

house. "Uncle Frank," he called.

In a few moments, they heard his crutches thumping against the hardwood floors.

"Ty boy, glad you are finally home. Katy was getting a little nervous about you not being back." He sat down in an over-stuffed chair in the sitting area.

Katy smiled up at Tyler. "Don't let Uncle Frank fool you. He was as concerned as I was. We hadn't heard a word from you since you left. We weren't sure what was going on."

"Hmm. Come with me." He led her into the office, to a machine on the credenza behind the desk. A red light flashed. "I guess I forgot to tell you about retrieving messages from the answering machine. Sorry 'bout that." He pushed a couple of buttons, and the device began to play taped messages.

"Hi, Katy. Just checking in to make sure everything is okay there and that you got my note. I really debated about waking you up, but it was so early, and I know you didn't get to bed until around three this morning. Anyway, I'm going to tie up all the loose ends I have in New York, and I should be back by day after tomorrow. I'll talk to you soon. Bye."

Tyler smiled at Katy. "Not calling you was never an option for me. I had to hear your voice, but somehow I kept missing you. Even Uncle Frank didn't answer the phone."

"I guess we were out when you called."

Tyler pushed another button. His voice sounded through the room. "Hi, Katy and Uncle Frank. I hope everything is okay there. I seem to keep missing you. Anyway, I've just left the city and will probably stop for the night in about eight hours and then be home by noon tomorrow. I miss you and can't wait to see you." He chuckled a second. "Yes, Uncle Frank, I miss you, too. See you soon."

"I only called those two times, but there's another message." He pushed the button.

"This is Keith Waters. I'm with Hobart Academy. I saw your ad in *Travel Today*. I'm glad to see you have reopened the ranch. My company has used your facilities for a week-long conference for our employees. Please give me a call at your earliest convenience."

"How cool is that? Our first reservations from the ad I did. WooHoo!" Tyler's enthusiasm washed over Katy. Her excitement matched his *woohoo* for *woohoo*.

Tyler took her in his arms, and she was quickly lost in the intimacy of their kiss. Although the intensity made her weak, her love for this man was stronger than anything she'd ever known. This was where she wanted to be for the rest of her life.

Circling his arms around her, Tyler crushed her body against his chest. Slowly, he moved his head back enough to look into her eyes. His lips were so close she could feel his breath on her lashes. Warm and inviting, she raised herself to his lips again, but he drew back enough to prevent her from kissing him.

"I hope I don't scare you away because you think I am crazy, but I have something I have to say. I know we've only known each other about two weeks, but I love you, Katy, more than I've ever loved anyone."

Her heart filled to bursting. Tyler Davis loved her. Her intuition hadn't been wrong. His body had told her the same things he had just said, and she had felt it all in every way possible. She wanted very much to tell him the same thing, but he cut her words short.

"You are everything I could ever look for in a woman. You're kind, smart, and beautiful and I know I can put my full trust in you. You've proven that to me."

As if struck with a Chinese gong, Katy bolted back out of his arms. "Tyler, I have to tell you something."

Gently he pulled her back to him. "I knew I would probably shock you, and I understand that. I don't expect you to love me back. Not yet anyway, but I had to tell you how I feel."

"But—"

He placed his fingertip to her lips. "I'm serious. I don't want you to commit to me until you are ready. And, if that doesn't happen, then I'll have to live with that, but for now I had to tell you my feelings."

When he pulled her to him again, Katy went willingly and savored the sweet taste of his lips. She didn't want to break the wonderful sphere of joy she and Tyler were locked in. Later she would tell him about her true identity, but for now she wanted to bond their love for each other.

The first time their lips parted, she whispered softly to Tyler, "I love you, too. I think I have from the moment I saw your cute little butt sticking out from under Old Blue's hood. And, if that didn't do it, Tweety bird on your underwear peeking out of a split in the back of your coveralls closed the deal."

After a few minutes of embracing and sealing their commitments with a kiss, Tyler and Katy went back into the sitting room where they'd left Uncle Frank.

"Where's George? He didn't come to meet me when I drove up." Tyler had become very fond of the hound.

"He hasn't been home in two days." A glint of mischief danced in the old man's eyes. "He's been chasing Moro's border collie. He may be an old dog, but when it comes to the females he thinks he's still a pup." Frank's infectious laugh rose from deep inside him.

Tyler looked a Katy, who smiled widely. "I guess love is in the air everywhere." He laughed for a few moments, then said to his uncle, "I have something to tell you," Tyler said to his uncle.

"Yeah, yeah, I know. You two are in love. If you'd asked me a while back, I could have told you that. You've reminded me of mine and Hildie's beginning. My father and mother had a barn dance here on the ranch. I took one look at Hildie on the arm of Buford Carey, and it was one of two things. Either we fell in love at first sight, or I would be damned before I let that jerk Buford Carey end up with a beautiful lady like my Hildie. Anyway, it worked out pretty good. You two will, too. What else you got to tell me?"

Tyler chuckled, pulled his wallet from his back pocket, and took out what looked like a bank check. He handed it to Frank.

"Whoa horsey! Where did you get that much money?"

"Believe me, it was not an easy task, but with Katy's help of putting the financial records for the ranch in order, and with the few funds I had stashed away, I was able to gather a good-sized chunk of it." Tyler put his arm around her and pulled her next to him.

"Then I took the engagement ring I'd bought for Beth back to the jeweler who sold it to me. He discounted it, of course, but that was another blast to pump up the total."

Hearing that the ring was gone was the final layer of faith for Katy in her new life. Joy bubbled through her.

"I'm still about ten thousand dollars short. I could take it out of the working funds for the ranch, but then we'd be struggling to cover salaries and expenses for the first reservations."

As if it were the most natural thing in the world, Tyler kissed Katy on the forehead. Her whole body tingled.

"I'm going to go take a shower." As he stepped away, warm air swirled around her, filling her with contentment.

"Then," Tyler continued, "I'm going into town to talk to the banker. I'm hoping he will take this much and allow us to pay the other ten thousand over a period of a couple of months. Surely, he'll be happy with ninety percent in one lump sum. Don't you think?"

"That's kinda hard to say, isn't it, Katy?" Frank looked at her.

The room grew quiet, and she shot Frank a questioning look. Why would he say such a thing? Did he know her secret? A chill slid down her spine.

"Is something wrong?" Tyler asked.

Frank glanced at Katy. "Nope, how can anything be wrong? You have saved the ranch, Ty boy."

"Okay. I'm going to get ready to go to town." He turned to Katy. "Would you like to go with me?"

"To take a shower?" Uncle Frank giggled like a school boy.

Tyler shot him one of those looks Katy had learned meant *I love you, old man, but you're a pill*. She knew it would be followed by laughter, and that was her favorite part.

"I think I'll pass on both counts. I still have several chores to get done." She raised herself on tiptoes and gave him a quick kiss. "Good luck with your mission. I'm going out to work in the rose garden. I'll see you when you get back."

Katy had to get out of there and get somewhere she could

think about the last hour. Tyler loved her, and she loved him, but what would he do when he found out who she really was and that she had lied to him all along? Her throat constricted painfully. She couldn't lose him now. She would tell him as soon as he returned from town.

With all her heart, she knew they were soul mates. Soul mates should encounter no problems that would be bigger than their love for each other. She counted on that. It had to be that way.

TYLER HAD showered and was just getting into the rental car when the foreman of the construction crew called to him. He walked to meet him.

"We cleaned out the water trough, and we found this." The man held out a cell phone with water still dripping out of it.

"Wonder how long that's been there?" Tyler pushed a few buttons and shook it, sending droplets of water in several directions."

"I don't have any idea, but my sister-in-law found one and took it to the store where the same kind was sold. The clerk was able to tell her who it belonged to."

"Really. That's interesting."

"Naw, the interesting part was that it belonged to a woman who worked with her husband. And she had found it in his truck."

"Oh, no."

"Oh, yes. And I think there's a store that sells that particular kind in the new strip mall on Main Street in Cantor."

"Well, I don't know what good it would do anyone now, but maybe there are numbers they can pull out of it to put into a new one. If I have time, I'll go by there. If it belongs to a former guest, I'm sure they'd like to know we found it, even if it no longer works. Thanks."

On the ride into town, Tyler enjoyed the most energizing breath of fresh air he'd taken in a long time. The heavy load that had been dumped on him was lightening more every day. He was pretty proud of all he'd accomplished in a few short weeks. He'd kept the crew going on the renovations Sidney had started and on the repairs which had to be done. Katy'd dug them out of a paper disaster that Tyler would never have found the bottom of. She'd put it all into a plan he could easily understand and know exactly where he stood in the large picture.

The thing that really made him the happiest was that he'd lost someone who really didn't love him, who had cheated on him, and had deceived him in every way possible. And while digging through the manure that had been his life lately, he'd found a well-fertilized rose. Katy.

There was no better feeling for Tyler than to know he loved her with everything in his heart, and, miracles of miracles, she loved him, too.

He saw the phone store tucked neatly in the corner of a strip mall. Once inside the store, he stepped up to the counter and handed the clerk the phone his foreman had given him.

"I found this in some water on my ranch. Do you have any way of determining who it belongs to? I hate to throw it away when maybe they have stored info in there that they can't retrieve anywhere else."

"Well, let's see." The clerk removed the back from the phone and then held it over a trash can behind the counter. Water drizzled out of it. He did some investigation, entered something into the computer, and in a matter of seconds he announced, "This belongs to Mays Savings and Loans. They're about two blocks down."

"Yeah, I know. I happen to be headed that way right now. I'll drop it off. Does this tell you to whom at the bank this belongs?"

"No, but here's the number. They should be able to figure it out." He scribbled the number on a small piece of paper and handed it to Tyler.

He drove the couple of blocks to the bank. He wasn't sure why he was so nervous. He supposed it was because so much hinged on him being able to convince K. T. Mays to accept the partial payment to stop the foreclosure on the ranch.

He straightened his tie and shined his boots on his pant leg. Ready as he would ever be, he opened the door and entered the bank. The first person he saw was Jeremy Everson. The two men shook hands.

"Thanks for doing that favor for me. I think it's going to work out," Tyler said.

"I'm glad. It's the least I can do."

Tyler handed him the cell phone and the scribbled phone number.

"I found this out on the ranch. When I checked with the phone store, they said it was registered to this bank, and this is the number that belongs to it. Any idea whose it is?"

Jeremy looked at the paper and then slowly lifted his gaze to meet Tyler's. Jeremy's odd look took Tyler aback. "This is Katy's phone."

"I don't understand. Why would Katy have a phone that belonged to Mays Savings and Loan?"

"Do you really not know that before she ended up at your ranch, she was the vice president in charge of loans and that she is Bill Mays' daughter?"

Chapter 16

IN THE LOBBY OF the Mays Savings and Loans Bank in Cantor, Georgia, would forever be the place where Tyler's world crashed down around him. Jeremy Everson informed him that Katy Mason was, in fact, *the* K. T. Mays, whose job it was to take the ranch away from Uncle Frank.

For the second time in three days, Tyler had learned that a woman who had professed to be in love with him had betrayed him and left him painfully aware that he was no judge of women, and evidently, never had been.

First Beth had stabbed him in the back, and now Katy had stabbed him in the heart. Numb with disbelief, Tyler struggled to keep the contents of his stomach from roiling. As shock gave way to rage, he forced himself to take control of the fire seething inside him and to take care of the business he'd originally came to the bank for.

He glowered at Jeremy, who took a hasty step backwards. "I'm sorry, man. I had no idea that info would come as news to you."

Tyler regretted his show of anger to the guy who had enlightened him to Katy's deceitful ways. After all, he was just the messenger.

"So you are saying that the K. T. Mays, who signed all the notices of foreclosure on the Dixie Rooster, is in fact Katy Mason, who has been working on the ranch for the past two weeks. Is that what I am to understand?"

"I'm afraid so."

Tyler took a deep breath, and with all that he held holy, shoved the thought of Katy to the back of his mind. "Who can I talk to about the mortgage on the ranch?"

Jeremy shrugged. "That would be Katy's dad, Bill Mays. If

you'll follow me, I'll show you to his office. And, again, I thought you knew." Jeremy led him to his boss's office. There he introduced Tyler to him, and then he made a rapid retreat from the room.

"What can I do for you, Mr. Davis?" Bill Mays motioned for Tyler to take a seat.

He started to refuse, but then called upon every fiber of professionalism within him. Once he was seated, and the noise in his head calmed to a roar, he handed Mays the cashier's check he'd brought with him from New York.

The banker opened a desk drawer and pulled out a file. Tyler assumed it held all the legal documents pertaining to the foreclosure. After flipping through several pages, Mays tossed the check back to Tyler's side of the desk.

"I'm afraid that isn't the full amount of the note." He locked his fingers across his stomach and leaned back in his chair.

"I know that it's a little short, but surely with me giving you that huge amount you can give us an extension on the last ten thousand dollars."

"Sorry, I can't do that."

"You can't or you won't?"

Mays leaned forward and rested his forearms on the desk. "Just because you have my daughter living on your ranch doesn't mean I'm going to give in on this matter." He picked up the cashier's check and held it out for Tyler to take. "The loan must be satisfied in full, and ten thousand dollars is a considerable amount from being *in full*."

Reluctantly, he took it. Disappointment centered in his chest. None of this could be happening. Surely he would wake up and find it was all a dream, but he knew it wasn't. Seated inside the car, he rested his aching head against the headrest and closed his eyes as tightly as possible.

The many thoughts racing through his mind sent shards of profound desperation in too many directions for him to even try to reason them out. He'd gathered every penny he could. There were no more funds available to him. So, in the end, Uncle

Frank's ranch would be taken from him, and Tyler could do nothing about it.

That alone was a painful blow to his chest, but coupled with learning that Katy had lied to him from day one, turned his heart into a tattered mess. And now he would have to go face her and tell her she was fired because he couldn't have a liar working on the ranch. Of course, that was now a moot point since, in two more weeks, there would be no ranch at all.

UNCLE FRANK AND Katy waited on the front porch for Tyler to return from the bank. He'd been gone plenty long enough to take care of the business in Cantor. She paced the length of the porch, and with each pass she felt Uncle Frank watching her.

Finally, he broke the silence. "You should have told him, Katy."

She stopped and stared his way. The look in his eye told her the jig was up. Somehow Frank Davis knew her secret.

"How long have you known?" Her dry mouth made it hard to speak.

"Since the day you got here." He pointed to the rocker next to him. "Have a seat. I've always banked in Augusta, but my bank wouldn't loan me and Sidney the money. For years, I trusted the man in charge at my home bank. His name is Tom Frazer."

"I know Mr. Frazer. He's a good man." Katy's voice sounded strange even to her.

"He always looked out for me. He advised me not to take out the loan in the first place, but I wanted to give Sid one more chance to prove what he was worth and maybe even make something of himself." Frank shook his head slowly. "I should have listened to Tom."

"I'm so sorry, Uncle Frank."

He laid his hand on Katy's and gave it a gentle squeeze. "I have a feeling that if you could have done anything about all this, you would've already."

"I really tried. I did some background checks on you, the ranch, and your son. I argued with my dad, which is something I never really did before. He wouldn't budge in his hard-headed ways." Katy exhaled a long sigh.

"The morning I came out here with the foreclosure notice, my dad said I had to serve the papers or find another job. When I saw the ad on the bulletin board, I knew it was something I could do, so I jumped at it. Maybe, in a way, I felt I was rebelling against my dad. That, too, was something I had never done. I'd always been the most obedient daughter anyone could ever ask for. I looked at this job as flying out of the nest."

"Better late than never." Frank smiled at Katy, and some of the fear lodged in her throat melted.

"You didn't tell me how you knew who I was."

"I'd been in your bank a couple of times during the process of getting the loan. Sidney had asked one of the tellers who you were. They told him and that you were engaged. Looks like you light up the hearts of all Davis men." Katy felt Frank's deep chuckle all the way to her heart.

When she looked at him, he nodded toward the entrance road. Tyler was back. Every nerve in her body throbbed painfully, and by the speed of the approaching car, she sensed he was furious.

Tyler slammed on the brakes so hard that the tires skidded another foot. Bounding out of the car, he raced up to Katy. "What kind of game is this you've been playing?"

"I'm sorry I didn't tell you my real name, but if I had, would you have hired me? No, you wouldn't have. When I took this job, I no longer worked for the bank."

"I find that hard to believe. If that were true, you would have told me who you are. Instead of searching through all our financial records and gathering anything you could to . . . to . . ."

Anger bordering on rage mixed with the ache from her full-blown broken heart and exploded inside Katy, forcing unwanted tears to stream down her face. Where had this pigheaded man come from? He certainly wasn't the same person who had held her gently and kissed her softly and declared his love for her. This Tyler was different and, at that moment, a little scary, but she refused to let him bully her. No one would ever do that to her again.

"You caught me, Tyler Davis. You foiled my diabolical plan to come here to the ranch, work my butt off to show you places you could recoup money to pay off the mortgage only to yank it away from you at the last moment. I'm guilty as charged. Aren't you glad you found out before you handed over all that money you came up with? Who knows? Heaven knows I had planned to stretch it out so that you would run out of time and lose the ranch anyway. Thank goodness you saw right through my conniving ways." Tears continued even after she'd finished her tirade.

Uncle Frank, who had quietly watched the rant of a woman on the verge of totally losing it, stood up. "I'm going inside so I don't get hurt if this goes to blows." He looked at his nephew. "Ty boy, how about using your head and your ears for something more than keeping your cowboy hat out of your eyes."

"Wait. I have to tell you something." Tyler stopped Frank. "Mays wouldn't accept the cashier's check. He wants all or nothing."

Katy released a low groan. "I was afraid that would happen."

Tyler glared at her and then opened the door for his uncle. Once the old man was safely inside, he faced Katy. "I don't know what your motive for lying was, but I do know I can't live with that. You need to get packed as fast as possible, and I'll run you into town."

"That won't be necessary. I'll leave the same way I came. I'll call Maria right now, and I'll be packed by the time she gets here." Katy went to the office to use the phone. Tyler followed her. While she called her friend, he put the cashier's check into an envelope and paper-clipped it inside the checkbook. Without a word or even looking at her, he left the room.

IT DIDN'T TAKE Katy long to gather all her belongings. She wished with all her might that she could leave her broken heart behind, but that would surely be with her for a long time. Although she'd been ordered to physically leave the ranch, it would be in her heart forever. She'd come to love this place almost as much as she loved Tyler.

On her way out the front door, she didn't see Uncle Frank or Tyler anywhere, but the light was on in the office. When she looked into the room, the checkbook lying out in the open grabbed her attention. Without another thought, Katy went around the desk and took the envelope holding the cashier's check.

She really didn't know if she would have better results than Tyler, but she knew for her own peace of mind, she had to try. She went onto the front porch and took a last look at the place she'd thought of as her home, even if it was only a short amount of time. Her gaze scanned the pastures, the stable, the rec room, and the cook shack. Each held a special memory for her, but bunkhouse number two held the sweetest of all. She placed her fingers to her mouth and could almost feel Tyler's lips on hers.

The jagged, painful thought of never being close to him again threatened to stop her heart. She steadied herself against the banister and then started walking down the long drive toward the highway. She couldn't bear being there another moment. When she glanced back, George was lumbering behind her. She'd tried to make him go back, but he refused. Katy relented and welcomed the dog's companionship on her lonely walk off the ranch.

MARIA DROPPED Katy off at her parents' home. She found her mother working in the garden. Shading her eyes, she looked up. "Katy." Her mother's voice was the sweetest sound she'd heard in a while. She rose and pulled her daughter into her embrace. "How are you?" Her mom released her tight hold long enough to look into Katy's eyes. "What's wrong? Are you okay?"

Katy rested her head on her mom's shoulder and through

heart-rending sobs she managed to say, "Nothing will ever be right again."

"Of course it will, sweetheart. Let's go in where it is cool, and we'll have some sweet tea."

Once inside the house she'd grown up in, and after her uncontrollable weeping subsided, Katy told her mom the whole story of the past two weeks.

"Did Dad get rid of my car?"

"No, of course not. It didn't matter that it is registered in the bank's name, it was a gift from your father and me to you for graduating into the working world."

"Then it would be okay if I took it?" Katy asked.

"Yes, but surely you aren't going out now. You just got here. We can work on dusting your room and putting clean sheets on your bed."

"No, Mom. I'm not coming back here to live. I have too many unsettled issues with Dad to stay here." She tugged her bottom lip between her teeth. "What I would like to do, just for a short time, is stay at the lake house. I promise I won't homestead it. I'll just be there until I make other decisions and arrangements. Will that be all right?"

Her mom rinsed out the tea glasses, placed them in the dishwasher, then dried her hands. "Sure. You can stay at the lake house."

"Thanks, Mom. I'll go on out there sometime today, but right now, I have to go to the bank and see Dad."

She gave her mom a quick hug, then plucked her car keys from the peg near the back door. She stopped and looked into her mother's large brown eyes. "I know about the engagement ring Dad bought and gave to Jeremy. Since you picked it out, you should know how much it cost. How much was it?"

Katy could tell her mom was searching for valid points to plead her case. "I don't need to hear anything about it except how much it is worth."

Her mom's shoulders sagged. "Right at six thousand dollars."

"Thanks," Katy said and left.

EVEN THOUGH IT had only been two weeks, it seemed a lifetime since Katy walked out of the bank. She nodded or waved to everyone who acknowledged her. Her dad's door was open, so she marched on in.

He didn't look at all surprised to see her. "Hello, Katlyn. I've been expecting you."

"I'll bet you have, but you need to know that the daughter who left here a couple of weeks ago isn't the same one standing here today."

She stepped closer to the desk. "I know you've always had a cold heart, but refusing to take the more than generous offering from the Davises and giving them time to pay off the last ten thousand dollars, is the most despicable thing you've ever done. You have no idea how hard they work, how deep their family roots are planted in that land you want to turn into a housing development." Katy had to swallow hard to dislodge the ball of anger in her throat. "It's just another example of how you bully everyone around you."

Bill Mays' face deepened to a purplish red. "You call it bullying, and I call it good business. That is what has bought you everything you ever wanted."

Katy shook her head adamantly. "No, Dad, that is what bought me everything *you* wanted me to have. What I wanted was a father."

"I was a good father to you and your wimpy brother. Your mom made both of you soft."

"Mom gave us all the love she had in her and still tried to give more to make up for what you didn't." Katy exhaled a disgusted sigh. "You were never a father. You've always been and continue to be a first-class bully. And because of that you've lost Aidan and now me."

Katy opened the envelope she'd hot fingered from the checkbook. She laid it on the desk, then stuck her hand in her pocket and pulled out her engagement ring. She placed it gently on top of the cashier's check. "You bought this ring so I could have the best. Well, this is what is best for me. Take this check and this ring, which I know is worth six thousand dollars, and apply it to the note for the Dixie Rooster. As for the remaining four thousand, you can either write it off, which we both know you have the capability to do, or set up monthly payments.

"If you think about it, you'll realize I never asked for anything, I never rebelled against your wishes even down to the person you wanted me to marry, but I am now. This one request will cover the hundreds I never even bothered to mention because I knew if it was something you wanted me to have, I would already have had it. Otherwise, it was out of the question.

"So, look at this any way you want, as a request, as a wish, or as a demand. I don't care, just so it gets done and gets done today."

Behind Katy, there was a slow and steady *clap, clap, clap*.

Before she spun around, she saw surprise on her dad's face. Quickly, she turned, and her voice clouded with tears. "Aidan, you've come home." She ran to her big brother, who picked her up and swung her around.

"Hey, Katydid. I sure have missed you." Aidan set her down and reached his hand across the desk. "Hi, Dad." There was an uncomfortable pause, but then the older man took his son's hand.

"It's good to see you, Aidan."

When Katy realized that was pretty much all the exchange the two hard-headed Mayses were going to do, she took it as a positive move and hoped there would be more soon.

She locked her arm through her brother's. "Let's go." She looked back over her shoulder. "Today, Dad. That has to be done today."

"Where are we going?" Aidan asked.

"You'll see." Katy pulled him out the door.

Chapter 17

IT HAD BEEN TWO long days since Tyler had stupidly told Katy she had to leave the ranch. He had no one to blame but himself for the pain that had been rifling through his body since her departure. How could he have let the best thing that ever happened to him march out the door and out of his life?

Sure, he was mad that she had lied about her name, and she was probably right on the mark when she said he wouldn't have hired her if he'd known who she was. But he had hired her, and he had fallen in love with her. And he believed with every scratch across his heart that she loved him.

They had even confessed to each other that they were soul mates. When Katy left two days ago, she had taken his soul with her.

Curse his pride. Curse his ego. Curse his stubbornness. They had all had a hand in his ruining the best thing that ever happened to him. They had all kept him from seeing that there was no way Katy had an ulterior motive. She'd worked hard, brought things to light in the financial status of the ranch and had even found lost money and had given Tyler ideas of how to raise even more.

How could he have been so pigheaded not to realize that other than the wrong name, nothing, absolutely nothing pointed to Katy being anything but honest and forthright. Tyler was pretty sure even Uncle Frank would have agreed she'd been the best thing to happen to the ranch in a long time.

Katy meant the world to Tyler, and because of his own ignorance he'd lost her for good. That very morning, he'd called Jeremy at the bank to see if he knew how to get a hold of Katy. Jeremy assured him that if he did, he would tell Tyler, but he didn't have a clue.

After Uncle Frank had relayed the story of Katy's father giving her an ultimatum, and she had chosen to quit her job at the bank to keep from telling Uncle Frank he had to vacate his land, Tyler could have kicked himself from the ranch to Augusta and back. It was too late for that. He'd screwed up everything, and he would have to live with it no matter how painful it was.

Rain had finally come to the Dixie Rooster and had cleaned away the dust from almost everything on the ranch. It had made everything like new, except for the sadness that had contaminated Tyler's life.

With the rain, there wasn't much outside work that could be done, but inside repairs were going well. Why he hadn't already put a stop to it all, he wasn't sure. He didn't know if it was because he owed so much to his uncle, and he didn't want to let him down. Or, was it because Katy had showed so much confidence in Tyler and had encouraged him to go for nothing less than restoring and saving the ranch? He didn't know. He only knew he loved Katy more than anything, even the ranch, and he was nothing without her.

Tyler forced himself to go out on the porch, sit in a rocker, and let the sound of the rain on the tin roof lull him into an afternoon nap. His dreams were filled with visions of Katy, and when he awoke, his eyes filled with tears.

Coming up the drive, a car bounced over the gravel and splashed through puddles. Tyler pulled his blue bandana handkerchief from his back pocket, blew his nose, and swiped at his eyes. Shortly Jeremy Everson got out of the car and ran for cover on the porch.

"Hi, Jeremy." Tyler rushed to meet him. "Have you found Katy?" Shaking and anxious, he nearly yelled at the poor man.

"Maybe, but right now I want to give you this." Jeremy handed Tyler some legal papers.

He glanced over them. "What is this?" he asked.

"It's a satisfaction of lien. I just had it recorded at the courthouse and wanted to make sure you got it as soon as possible."

Dumbstruck, Tyler asked, "How did this happen?"

"Day before yesterday, Katy paraded into her dad's office and paid off the mortgage."

Tyler couldn't make the vision of that happening come into focus in his mind. "Just like that? Where did she get the money?"

"I really can't say. I guess you'll have to ask her."

Running his fingers through his hair and exhaling loudly, Tyler couldn't wrap his mind around any of it. "I'm so confused. How can I ask her that when I don't know where she is?"

"I had an idea, so I checked it out, and I was right. I was sworn to secrecy, so I can't tell you where she is."

Tyler gripped his hands into fists and struggled with his need to punch something, but he managed to stay in control. "You have to tell me where she is."

"I told you I can't, but, and you didn't hear this from me, I have a feeling her mother will tell you. Go see her." Jeremy handed Tyler a business card with a name and address handwritten on the back of it. He assumed that was where he could find Katy's mother.

He took Jeremy's offered hand and shook it graciously. "Thanks for everything. By the way, do you know if Aidan got in contact with Katy?"

Jeremy smiled widely. "Oh, yeah, in grand style. Go see Mrs. Mays in person. I'm sure she'll guide you in the right direction." The sound of his chuckle floated back to Tyler. That coupled with the unexpected satisfaction of the lien on the ranch lightened the misery he'd been dealing with for two days.

How had Katy managed to do away with the threat of foreclosure? Suddenly, he thought of the cashier's check. Hurriedly, he ran into the office and snatched the checkbook open. The envelope was gone. Katy had taken it and probably put her own money with it to satisfy the full amount.

After a few seconds of over-thinking how all that had happened, Tyler came to the conclusion that Katy had taken a check that didn't belong to her, but she had added her own money to it and paid off the ranch loan. How could Tyler find fault in any of that? If anything, he now had more proof that Katy loved the ranch and would do what was necessary to save it.

With the same determination, Tyler silently affirmed his love for Katy, and he would do whatever it took to get her back.

Like a bolt of lightning, he raced out of the office and down the hallway to Uncle Frank's room. He'd been hiding out in there, and Tyler was pretty sure it was because he had screwed up the best thing that had ever happened to him, and Uncle Frank was pretty ticked.

"What is it?" The old man roused from his sleeping position in the recliner.

"Katy somehow managed to pay off the loan. The ranch is free and clear again. You're back in business."

"Yeah, well that's good, but it still won't mean as much without her here." Frank glared at his nephew.

"I'm going to take care of that. I'm going to go find her and bring her back, even if I have to hog tie her."

"Whoa there, cowboy. I think a little sweet talk and a lot of groveling will work much better. And while you are at it, tell her I kinda think a whole heapin' bunch of her, too. Sure would like to see her back before breakfast."

"You bet. Be back as soon as possible."

My plan is to have her back here by bedtime.

TYLER DROVE Old Blue down the narrow trail until he came to a sign that read *Bill's Hideaway*. There he turned into a gravel drive and soon came to a two-story log cabin just like Katy's mother had said he would. Even though it was early in the afternoon, the gray rain clouds cast dark shadows over the house and the lake behind it.

There was no car, but a light glowed through a downstairs window. Inside he could see a television playing, but no one moved within his sight. Tyler sucked in a fortifying breath, slipped on his cowboy hat, and ran from the truck to the front door. He banged the brass door knocker several times. Rain pooled on his hat, then dripped off the brim over his lightweight shirt. A chill danced its way through him. This time he rapped sharply on the door glass.

The door swung open, and Katy jolted to a stop. Surprise clearly showed on her face.

"I thought you were someone else. What do you want?" Her voice was nearly as cold as the rain.

"First, I'd like to get out of this terrible weather."

She hesitated. For a moment Tyler thought she was going to refuse to let him in, but a second later she stepped aside and motioned for him to enter. He removed his hat, and she took it and hung it on a hall tree.

"I ask you again, Tyler, what do you want?"

"I have so many things to say, I'm not sure where to start."

"Well, pick a place and jump in."

"Okay, thank you for whatever you did to save the ranch." Instantly, Tyler was lost in her shining brown eyes that oddly reminded him of the root beer barrel candy he'd loved as a child.

"You're welcome." Katy broke his reverie.

Quickly, he came back from that place in his heart where nothing had stood in the way of their love. "And, by the way, how did you come up with the last ten thousand?"

"That doesn't matter. It was something I wanted to do for Uncle Frank so he could see that I love the ranch, and I would never do anything to stop him from having it back in his family."

"Funny thing about that is Uncle Frank knew that all along. I was the only hardheaded person who needed more time to be convinced of that. I'm not handing out excuses. I'd just gathered the shattered pieces of my ego back from a woman who deceived me in so many ways. I thought that lightning had struck twice."

He moved closer to her. She didn't back away, and Tyler took that as a good sign. Was there a chance she would forgive him? He had to believe that.

"Katy, you have to forgive me for being so thick-headed. I didn't mean to hurt you, but I couldn't get past the one thing I never thought I'd have to face with you. You lied. And even though I agree with your reasoning behind it, at that moment, it threw a roadblock in front of my rational thinking. I'm sorry for that, and I can't erase it." He took her hands in his. "But I can work double time to make it up to you. And I will."

Tyler moved close enough to pull her into his embrace, but waited for a sign from Katy that she would not shy away.

"I love you, Katy. There has never been another woman who made me feel the way you do. The Dixie Rooster is so close to being ready for the guests who have reservations in two weeks. So much of that is thanks to you. We would never have made it this far without you. Please say you'll forgive me, and you'll come back to the ranch to stay."

Just then, the door burst open, and in came Katy's soaked brother. She pulled a throw from the back of a living room chair and tossed it to him. "Good heavens, Aidan. You're soaked. Put this around you."

Katy took the two bags of groceries from him and hurried them to the kitchen. Hearing Tyler and Aidan talking, she hurried back to make their introductions, but found that wasn't necessary. They were talking like they were old friends.

"Excuse me, but do you two know each other?" She looked first at Aidan, who sent a questioning glance to Tyler.

"You haven't told her?" he asked.

"She's been so mad at you for the last two days, I didn't dare bring up your name." Aidan smiled his cockeyed grin.

Katy knew she was being left out of the joke. "Okay, that's enough. One of you tell me what's going on."

Tyler was the first to speak. "I never had a brother or sister, and it broke my heart to hear you talk about Aidan disappearing from your life. I took a chance that Jeremy might be able to help me locate him. And, by the way, Jeremy's not such a bad guy. He called Aidan and had him call me. I told him you were staying at the ranch, and I told him he was welcome to come and visit with his sister any time he liked."

Katy's painful heart healed a little. She looked at her brother.

"It only took a day to get my leave approved," Aidan said. "When I got to town, I decided I needed to go see Dad and basically tell him how much he'd hurt me and Mama and you, but when I arrived, my baby sister was giving him hell." He looked at Tyler. "You should have seen her. I think she put Dad into shock. He said very little. What's that saying? Gasoline to drive there, fifty-two dollars? Look on Dad's face, priceless."

So it was Tyler who had contacted her big brother and brought him home, even if it was for just a visit. Even if his leave from the Army would be over in two more days, it was Tyler she had to thank for her time with Aidan.

But Tyler had accused her of some pretty tough stuff, and she wasn't sure she could forgive him for the way he made her feel like the most precious thing in his life one day and a few days later tell her to leave the ranch because he couldn't trust her. Love doesn't change or get washed away that quickly. Katy wasn't sure she could trust him not to break her heart so completely again without giving her time to explain or for him to give her the benefit of the doubt.

Her mind and heart didn't work like that. To her, love was the boundary for a relationship. It was the love that held you inside that circle where you worked out your disagreements, doubts, and problems. But never, ever did you allow anything to push you outside the love. Sadly, she wasn't sure Tyler could do that, and she wasn't sure she could continue to go through the living hell she'd been in since he'd banished her from the ranch.

"This silence is deafening. I'm going to start cutting up the veggies for the salad. You two go out on the lanai and duke it out until you are ready to kiss and make up."

Katy shot Aidan a glare that should have killed a normal person, but he just ignored her.

"And Katydid, just a word of advice—move those pigtails away from your ears so you can hear every word Tyler says, because whether you know it or not, this man loves you and you love him. That should be the most important part."

"That's funny. That is almost word for word what Uncle Frank said to me." Tyler took Katy's arm, and she allowed him to lead her to the back porch.

The rain had slowed some, but the cool damp air chilled her. Tyler pulled her next to him. "I love you, Katy. Please tell me you will come back to the ranch. I want you with me. I know you love me. Please say yes."

"I was wrong not to tell you my true identity, and I admit it was for selfish reasons. At first I just wanted any job other than the one I had at the bank, but in a very short amount of time, I fell in love with every inch of the ranch. I was afraid that when I told you, I would be sent away. My fears were right. You did send me away and severed any emotional strings we had. It was snip, snip, and I was gone from your life. I can't live with that."

"And you don't have to. I'm not saying I won't ever do anything stupid, but you can count on the fact that I'll never send you away again, no matter what the reason."

And while he waited patiently, Katy took her sweet time as she sorted through and pitched out every raw emotion she'd felt in the last couple of days. When she was sure there was nothing left, she ran into Tyler's arms and held onto him with all her might.

"I love you Tyler, and right now I want your promise that no matter what stumbling block comes our way, we will fight our way past it together and keep our eye on the most important thing—our love for each other."

"I'll promise if you tell me something. How did you settle the last of the money for the loan?"

"When Jeremy came to the ranch that day, I found out he had not bought my engagement ring. My father had. He wanted it to be the best. That day, Jeremy gave it back to me. So, when I took Dad your cashier's check, I gave him back the ring he'd bought for me and told him to apply it toward the remaining ten thousand. The ring wouldn't completely cover it all, so I told him to either take a loss on it or set up a payment plan for the remainder."

"Since you used the money from Beth's engagement ring, and I used mine, too, you might consider adding a tagline to the ranch's logo. *The Dixie Rooster Ranch, the ranch saved by two engagement rings.*"

Epilogue

Five Months Later

COOL, CRISP AUTUMN air blew across the Dixie Rooster Ranch. From the porch, Katy watched the latest group of guests depart. There would be a two-day break before the next ones arrived. Across the driveway, she saw the three housekeepers bustling from one bunkhouse room to another, taking soiled linens and towels to the washers located in the huge storage room behind the cook shack.

Several ranch hands were working in the stables. She suspected Tyler was there, too, because his beautiful blue truck with rooster decals on the door sat next to the corral. A month before, he'd got the call that the truck belonging to the ranch had been recovered, and Sidney was being held in a jail in Albuquerque, New Mexico.

Uncle Frank wouldn't press charges, but he wanted the truck back. After a few days of many phone calls to the storage yard that had picked it up, and after collecting notarized proof of ownership and a hold harmless agreement so Uncle Frank couldn't come back on the company for any damages or anything that went wrong once they released it, and then faxing the whole mess to the towing yard, it was finally ready to be put on a car carrier and brought back to the ranch.

According to Tyler, it was a fine ride, and, in the end, he was grateful his cousin had great taste in trucks.

Standing there, surveying the lay of the land and all it had to offer, Katy's body came alive with the joy only Tyler could give her. She appreciated the swirl of cool air blowing across her warm flesh, but most of all she cherished the tall, handsome man who had given up his northern, big city connections to return to his southern roots. She loved her Dixie Cowboy and always would.

As if her thoughts conjured him up, Tyler came out of the stable and into the bright sunlight. Leading two saddled horses, he motioned for Katy to come to him, which she gladly did.

When she reached Tyler, he handed her Shiloh's reins. "Let's go for a ride."

"Great. Where are we going?"

"It's a surprise. Just follow me," Tyler said.

As they rode over the first rise in the back pasture, Katy knew where they were headed. She could see the original homestead long before they reached it. Surrounding the house, the kudzu had mostly turned brown and was nothing more than vines twisted together as if bound forever. Just the way she wanted to be with Tyler.

Someone had been working hard on stripping the old house of the creeping plant, and Katy could see that much of the original structure was still intact. The front section of the roof had caved in, but the façade still stood tall and proud.

Katy stopped at the carriage step and slid down from her saddle. "Did you clear this away?" she asked.

Tyler grinned from ear to ear. "I had help. As soon as Uncle Frank had his cast removed, he declared this was his project."

From the history notebook she'd been reading, she already knew this home had held wonderful special memories for the past generations of Davises. For several minutes she stared in awe, imagining children playing on the large porch, and she could almost hear their laughter.

"Uncle Frank and I were both amazed at how much of the old house is still sound. I hope to make it livable for you and me to spend the rest of our life in."

Katy pulled her gaze away from the house to look at Tyler, who was looking up at her from a kneeling position. He took her hand. For a second, she couldn't feel her heart beating. It was quiet, as if it wanted to hear every word Tyler said.

"Katlyn Mays, I love you with all my heart. I want nothing more than for you to be my wife, my partner in life, and the mother of my children. And I can't see any of that happening anywhere else than right here."

Tyler opened a small box that held the most beautiful ring Katy had ever seen.

"Katy, will you marry me?"

Without hesitation she answered, "Yes. A thousand times, yes."

Tyler rose and placed the ring on Katy's finger, then he lifted her into his arms and spun her around. Once he'd set her back down, she held out her left hand and admired the gorgeous, unusual ring.

"This is beautiful. I've never seen one like it." There were three small circles. The center one held a brilliant solitaire diamond. Each of the other two circles placed on either side held a small diamond.

Tyler pointed to the largest. "That represents our love for each other, our love of family, and our love for the ranch. The two that flank the middle one represent the two engagement rings that saved the ranch."

Katy threw her arms around Tyler's neck. "I love it. I love what it represents and more than anything else, I love you, and I can't wait to be your wife."

They shared a soft, gentle kiss to seal their pact to spend the rest of their lives together.

"You want to go in and look around?"

"Absolutely. I need to see how many bedrooms there are so I'll know how many children we have room for."

"I believe I heard at some point in my life, there were six bedrooms in the old house."

"Six bedrooms?"

"Yeah, but don't worry, we can add more if we need them."

Coming in 2014

Book 2 of The Dixie Cowboys Series

Dixie Baby

Acknowledgements

Special thanks to Vickie King and Marge Smith my long-time friends who encourage me every day to write what's in my heart, but never let our friendship stand in the way of passing along strong (and almost always right) critiques of my work. I'm thankful for the important roles they play in my life.

About the Author

DOLORES WILSON has a long list of things she likes to do. Reading, cooking for friends and family, and traveling with her husband Richard in their motorhome to car shows and bluegrass/gospel festivals, but her biggest pleasures come from her grandkids and writing stories that swim through her mind every day.

She was transplanted from her hometown in Morgantown, West Virginia at the age of ten to Tampa, Florida. There she met her husband and two of her three children were born. Her third child was born in Jacksonville, Florida where Dolores resides today, surrounded by her adult children and grandkids.

Dolores is multi-published in women's fiction. The first book in her Sweet Meadow series, BIG HAIR AND FLYING COWS, was nominated for the Publishers Weekly Quill Award as one of the top 100 humorous books in the United States. She truly was honored to be among so many great humorous writers like Dave Barry and Jon Stewart, who won the award that year.

She is a member of Romance Writers of America and an active member of Ancient City Romance Authors. Be sure to visit Dolores' website at www.doloresjwilson.com for the latest news on releases, contests, and links to several blogs, including her blog of her trip to Alaska (2013). She loves to hear from readers, and she answers all emails.

CPSIA information can be obtained at www.ICGtesting.com
Printed in the USA
LVOW12s1135260114

371016LV00001B/175/P

9 781611 943740